"Oh, Michael, all women are not like that—we're not!"

He looked up at her then, and caught the hand that had moved to his face. "No," he said slowly, "you're not like that. I've never known a woman like you, never let myself know any woman. You're generous, you're bright, you're fun, and you laugh like a man!" His own laughter was low and delighted as he held her face in his hands and looked into her eyes.

Faintly she said, "I'm not sure…is that a compliment?"

"Oh, you can be sure of it! Brenna, lovely Brenna, I cannot keep my promise any longer."

She felt absolutely powerless, not against the dark-eyed man whose lips touched her face so gently, then moved inexorably to her mouth, but against the floodtide of longing within herself. For several endless, blissful moments she knew only that she wanted nothing but for this to go on forever.

Dear Reader,

The Cherish Romance™ you are about to read is a special kind of romance written with you in mind. It combines the thrill of newfound romance and the inspiration of a shared faith. By combining the two, we offer you an alternative to promiscuity and superficial relationships. Now you can read a romantic novel—with the romance left intact.

Cherish Romances™ will introduce you to exciting places and to men and women very much involved in today's fast-paced world, yet searching for romance and love with commitment—for someone to cherish and be cherished by. You will enjoy sharing their experiences. Most of all you will be uplifted by a romance that involves much more than physical attraction.

Welcome to the world of Cherish Romance™—a special kind of place with a special kind of love.

Etta Wilson

Etta Wilson, Editor

Irish Lace

Patricia Dunaway

Cherish Romances

Thomas Nelson Publishers • Nashville • Camden • New York

FOR CHRIS
A true friend is a gift of God.

Published in Nashville, Tennessee, by Thomas Nelson,
Inc. and distributed in Canada by Lawson Falle, Ltd.,
Cambridge, Ontario.

Printed in the United States of America.

Scripture quotations are from the Holy Bible: New International
Version. Copyright © 1978 by the New York International Bible So-
ciety. Used by permission of Zondervan Bible Publishers.

Both the poetry quotation on page 55 from "The Lover Tells of the
Rose in His Heart" and the one on page 56 from "When You Are
Old" are taken from *The Poems of W. B. Yeats*, edited by Richard J.
Finneran (New York: Macmillan, 1983).

All of the characters in this book are fictitious. Any resemblance to
actual persons, living or dead, is purely coincidental.

ISBN 0-8407-7350-1

Chapter One

They say that people who live near mountains claim them as their own; very possessively they will speak of *my* mountains. Brenna stared dreamily at the dozen peaks known as the Twelve Bens, looming protectively over the little village of Clifden. Having been born and raised in the flat land of south Texas, she was fascinated by the Bens. All of the rolling Irish countryside charmed her, with its ever-changing patchwork of dark and light greens and flashes of gold from the sun making its way to the west behind her. What had the tour guide said? "The next parish is America...."

She sat a long time, perhaps too long, on the low stone wall. The faraway, late afternoon mist, creeping from the purpling mountains, had made its way among the mossy stones beneath her. Reluctantly she rose, drawing in deep, unhurried breaths of the soft Irish air. The blue haze surrounding the mountains carried with it the tang of the Atlantic Ocean and peat smoke, she was sure, although she'd never smelled peat smoke before.

Now, should I continue on down Sky Road or go back toward Clifden to find the O'Riordans, she mused. *It's so lovely....*She had picked up her shoulder bag, and pulled on one sleeve of her corduroy jacket, when suddenly a rabbit skittered frantically across the narrow road. Brenna was searching the grassy slope beyond the stone wall for the small creature so she missed seeing the young sheep dog bound onto the road. But the thud she heard behind her was unmistakable. She turned, dreading what she might see, hoping she was wrong.

She wasn't. The driver of a small green car had braked and clambered out. They reached the injured dog at about the same moment. Heedless of her dark blue slacks Brenna dropped to her knees in the wet gravel and gently stroked the dog's head. The fine-plumed tail wagged slightly at her touch. "Is he badly hurt, do you think?"

The man who knelt beside her shook his head. The distress was plain on his face. "I cannot tell, and I didna see him, either. Ran out, he did."

"He was chasing a rabbit." Brenna crooned softly to the whining dog, "There, there." She looked up at the man. "We have to do something!"

"Aye, we must. I'll take him to Crosswinds."

"Crosswinds?"

"Yup. Been called that since before Larkin ever bought it, and that's been thirty year or more. Some fine English lady built it and thought it ought to have a fancy name," the sarcasm was heavy in his tone, "and so it became."

"Who is Larkin?" She tried to keep the anxiety from her voice.

"He's the vet'nary. Well, there's two, you know, father and son. Only a stone throw to the village, luckily."

"I..." Brenna hesitated. Living in a city the size of Houston had made her cautious, but the honest concern for the dog in the man's face reassured her. "I'd like to go with you, to see how badly he's hurt—if you don't mind, that is."

6

The glance that swept from her thick black hair to the blue eyes wide now in her pale, rather anxious face, to the soft blue sweater and trim slacks appraised her frankly but seemed guileless. "A softie for dogs, are you?" he asked with an open smile.

She nodded. "And horses, and cats, but I guess especially dogs. Can I help move him?"

"Nae, lass. I'll get the poor chap in. If you'll just open the door of m'car?" Swiftly, efficiently he scooped the dog up with the flat palms of his hands and carried him quite as carefully as Brenna would have herself.

When the animal was placed on the seat between them, they set off down the road. "I'm MacGill, and who might you be? This is rather a late hour, and I'd not expected to see an American tourist, especially such a pretty one, when I set off this evening."

She heard the question *What in the world are you doing out here alone?* in his words. "I'm Brenna Ryan, and I—"

He interrupted her with a chuckle. "Well, that's an Irish lassie's name, but spoken with a right quare accent, for sure."

She smiled. "Mine may be queer, but yours is marvelous." There'd been a lot of comments about her Texas drawl since she'd left home, so she took the stranger's jabs with good grace. "How far is it to the vet's?" she asked, for the dog stirred and moaned just then.

"Not to worry, we're here. And we're in luck, for I see young Michael's just pulled in. Some of the old ones say he's not the vet his father is, but I'd trust him any day." As they came to a stop, MacGill leaned out the window and called, "Eh—Young Michael, we've a patient for ye!"

To her mild surprise, the man who got out of the battered blue Austin reminded Brenna instantly of her brother. As he walked toward them she could see the same unruly black hair and deep-set eyes, the same rangy body that her brother Sam punished regularly in every weekend rodeo he could find. This man was not as tall, however, and didn't have Sam's easy, open smile. His face wore a serious, almost solemn expression that instinctively she knew was habitual.

"MacGill," he nodded. "What have you there?" At the sight of the dog on the seat he said simply, "What happened?"

"The dog just ran in front of me—chasin' a rabbit he was. I couldna miss him for I never even saw him."

MacGill stepped out and moved aside as the younger man leaned into the car, his eyes intent on the dog. With long, slender fingers he carefully stroked and explored the dog's limp body. Brenna watched, fascinated by the gentle expertise of the strong hands, the absolute absorption on his somber face as he murmured, "There, there, fellow, we'll soon have you right again."

MacGill gave a little sigh. "The young lady here was takin' the air on the road when it happened. She's that concerned about the pup, I'll say that. Wanted to come along to see how badly he was hurt."

"Yes. Well, let's get him round to the surgery." Michael Larkin picked up the dog as carefully as MacGill had, pausing only long enough to nod in Brenna's direction. "If you'd like to wait inside you may, Miss. My father is probably in a raging snit because his tea is late, but perhaps he'll be civil." His expression said, *And perhaps not.*

Both men busied themselves then in moving the dog inside to the clinic at the rear of the house. Brenna got out of the car and stood uncertainly for a moment after they had disappeared around the side of the house. Turning toward the front, she saw a fair example of

Georgian colonial, although the dwelling had seen better days. The arched portico and entryway were framed by a graceful fanlight above and slender sidelights. Each flanked by dark green shutters, four sash windows on the first floor and four above gave a pleasant sense of symmetry. Two brick chimneys rose precisely between them. As Brenna shivered a bit, feeling the oncoming chill of evening, she noticed that an inviting, warm glow poured out through the drawn curtains in two of the downstairs windows.

Her feelings were mixed. Concern for the injured dog was uppermost, but there was a curious, underlying sense of pique at having been completely and royally dismissed by Michael Larkin. The somber young veterinarian was quite possibly the best looking man she'd ever seen. She told herself he'd been intent on seeing to the dog, but she also had to admit he hadn't so much as glanced at her when he'd said she could wait inside.

For lack of a better plan she went to the door at the front and twisted the old-fashioned doorbell. There was a loud thump, an incomprehensible shout, then silence. She hesitated, then rang the bell again.

"Come!" came the shout, clear this time.

Brenna took a deep breath, opened the door, and slipped in.

"Well, don't just stand out there," a sharp male voice boomed through the entry hall. "Show yourself!"

She did as she was bidden and came face to face with an elderly man ensconced in a maroon plush chair, his left leg straight out before him on a footstool that was drawn close to a welcoming fire.

"And who might you be?" he demanded.

"I'm Brenna Ryan, and—"

"What are you doing here, anyway?"

"Well, I was looking for the O'Riordans, sir. A girl in

9

the village told me they live somewhere near here. I guess I'm sort of lost."

"Likely as not you didn't follow instructions properly. Most women can't follow their own noses. No sense of direction." He scowled and moved his leg a fraction.

"You may be right," said Brenna, intimidated in spite of herself. Even seated he was quite formidable, with his piercing black eyes, bushy gray brows and hair. "At any rate, I happened to see Mr. MacGill hit a dog and we brought it here to be treated. Your son told me to come inside to wait while he and Mr. MacGill took the dog around to the surgery. I'm terribly sorry to have bothered you, sir. Please excuse me." Brenna turned to go.

"Wait! Where are you going?" he rapped out.

Startled, she found herself stammering. "To…to find the O'Riordans. I understood they have bed and breakfast accommodations, and I need a place to stay tonight."

"They live four houses toward town, on the *other* side of the road," he said pointedly. "Can you make tea?" he asked, startling Brenna again with his abrupt change of subject.

"Why, yes, I suppose so."

"If you saw Michael outside, he'll be in shortly and will be wanting tea as much as I do. There was a girl here this afternoon," he closed his eyes at an obviously painful memory, " 'hoped she might work out, but she was worse than the last one who applied for the job. Blast that silly Nola, anyway. A man ought not have to wait for his tea…" Muttering oaths under his breath, he eyed her from under the bushy brows as she stood still in amazement. "Put boiling water in the pot first, to warm it up. Second shelf on the right above the sink, the brown one with blue stripes. Just be sure the kettle's at the boil when you pour it over the leaves, eh? And use plenty of tea. Can't abide a stingy woman." When Brenna still did not move he said carefully, a semblance of a smile now on his brown, seamed face, "The kitchen's down that hall. Please?" he added as though he was down to the last resort: politeness.

Somewhat dazed, Brenna glanced around the cozy room; it was a comfortable hodgepodge of furnishings, from an ornate Victorian loveseat to a couple of sturdy, homemade tables. Every available surface was covered with magazines and periodicals, books and trivia. Another chair opposite Mr. Larkin's was a deep blue with squares of ancient-looking tapestry on the back and arms. The lamps were lit, and the fire burned brightly. It was altogether a pleasant room. She decided quite suddenly that she wanted to wait and hear about the dog anyway, and she could do with a cup of something hot even if she did have to make it herself. Determinedly she smiled and said, "Coming right up, sir. Tea it is!" Then she headed down the hall to find the kitchen.

Seamus Larkin grudgingly called Brenna's pot of tea "fair." Over his second cup he gave a little sigh of satisfaction and asked bluntly, "Now supposin' you tell me why you're wandering about at near dark alone, looking for O'Riordans."

Brenna tried to gauge his interest and decided it was genuine. She took a deep breath and plunged in. "When my friend Leslie and I got off the tour bus in Clifden today, I had the most unusual feeling..." She trailed off, then began again. "Well, the pace of the tour has been really frantic the past couple of days, and when I saw your lovely village, and smelled the sea air and the peat smoke..." Her voice grew dreamy at the memory.

"Go on," he prompted gruffly.

"It's simple, really. I decided I wanted to stay here a few days and told the guide to take my things off the bus. Leslie was flabbergasted when I said I didn't want to finish the tour—she told me I was being silly, but it was what I wanted to do, so I did it."

"Just like that, eh?" She nodded, and his bushy brows lowered. "Do you often do things on the spur of the moment, girl?"

"The funny thing is, I never do. But I don't regret it at all." She made a little face and added, "At least I wouldn't if I could find a place to stay. I hope the O'Riordans have a room for me."

"Hm. I begin to see your situation. A bit ticklish, wouldn't you say?" He cut loose then with another colorful expletive, and Brenna ducked her head in spite of herself. "What's wrong, girl, your ears tender?"

Not really wanting to say anything, Brenna murmured something unintelligible.

"Speak up, girl, say what's on your mind!" Seamus said. "I certainly do."

"Well, it make me uncomfortable when you use God's name like that," she said honestly.

"Humph. You're one of those religious women, I take it." The way he spoke made her think "religious" was the worst thing a woman could be.

"That depends on what you mean by 'religious.' I am a Christian, and when I say His name I use it more …carefully."

"And I suppose you want me to be careful, too," he said ominously.

"Yes, I'd feel better if you did."

"Ha! You sit in my house, by my fire, drinking my tea, and you have the audacity to tell me how I'm supposed to speak?"

12

Brenna, warming to the battle, had opened her mouth to reply when Michael Larkin entered the doorway. His shoulders slumped with weariness. Though he probably was not quite six feet tall, his rangy, long-limbed body gave the impression of a much taller man. Fleetingly Brenna thought that her dad would have labeled him hungry-looking. The shock of curly black hair, the black eyebrows and eyes so brown they too looked black, made her think of the term *black Irish*. His dark eyes barely acknowledged her as he sank into the blue chair opposite his father and leaned back wearily on the cushion.

"How's the hurt pup?" asked Seamus.

"Broken front leg."

"Set it all right?"

"Yes. It was a clean break. MacGill thinks perhaps it's Rankin's dog and went to tell him." He stretched his legs out on the footstool. "I'm done in."

"Bad delivery at Murphy's?" Seamus asked sympathetically.

Michael nodded. "Lost the calf."

A grunt of commiseration from Seamus. "Called too late; Murphy always does, then expects a miracle. Breech?"

A nod from Michael.

Another grunt from Seamus. "Young cow, I'll wager."

"First calf. Maybe her last."

"Too bad."

Brenna stared at the two men in absolute amazement. For all practical purposes she might as well have not even been in the room. She cleared her throat. "Would you like some more tea, Mr. Larkin?" Glancing at Michael Larkin, she thought him possibly the rudest man she'd ever met, except maybe Seamus Larkin.

"Yes, that'd be good, girl. And make some sandwiches for Michael. Lose 'em or not it's hard work, calving is." He nodded his head in sympathy. "Meat's in the fridge. Cheese, too. Use plenty of butter."

As though she were in a daze Brenna rose and moved from the room. Part of her astonishment was in reaction to the utter audacity of the old man, but for the most part, she was shocked at her own compliance. As she made her way down the hall to the kitchen Seamus Larkin bellowed, "And be sure the kettle's at the boil!"

At least the kitchen's pleasant, she thought as she searched for sandwich ingredients. There was plenty of evidence of a woman's touch here: blue gingham curtains hung at the window and polished copper utensils brightened the space above the formidable black stove. She found crusty, high loaves of homemade bread wrapped securely in a white enameled bread box, its curved front embellished with blue Delft designs.

As she sliced the bread and buttered it thickly, the kettle began to whistle merrily. Brenna found it difficult to believe she was in a charming old house in Ireland fixing supper for two not-so-charming Irish veterinarians. *This isn't exactly your average vacation schedule*, she admitted wryly to herself. The evening was more like being home and preparing supper for her father and younger brother, before her father had remarried and Sam left home for college—except Michael Larkin was far from being her brother!

She arranged the sandwiches attractively, poured boiling water over the generous batch of tea leaves and, picking up the tray easily, squared her shoulders and marched back into the cozy room. Neither man looked up, but when she placed the tray on the table between them Michael took a sandwich and began to eat as though he hadn't seen food in two days. Between bites he asked, "Where the deuce is Nola, anyway?"

Brenna stared at him, indignation rising in her alarmingly. Before she could speak, however, Seamus was already in conversation. "Nola is off on one of her secret missions without a word as to when she'll return. But I, my boy, have just had a brilliant idea."

"Excellent. I'm certainly too tired to be brilliant." Michael reached for another sandwich, still not looking at Brenna.

Brenna had had enough. "Mr. Larkin," she began, looking straight at the younger man, "Since I've been in your home I've been shouted at, ordered around, both of you have been unbelievably rude, and I'm not real sure I believe everything I've heard about Irish hospitality and friendliness any more. In fact, you all are just impossible!" She sputtered, dismayed that, as always, her Texas accent reached abominable heights when she was angry.

Both men stared at her. Michael spoke first, slowly, and he was definitely looking at her now. "You're absolutely right. Seamus and I are not always civilized—Mrs. O'Malley often says so. She also says it's the lack of a feminine presence here at Crosswinds that is responsible, but I'm not convinced that's true."

Brenna bit back an acid comment. "Well, if the dog is going to be all right, I'll go now—"

"Wait," broke in Seamus, "You haven't heard my idea." He cocked his bushy gray head toward Brenna. "How much cash money do you have with you, girl? Enough?"

"Why, I—" Brenna stopped. Something in Seamus Larkin's eyes somehow inspired the need to be truthful, in spite of his rudeness. "No, probably not. I have no idea how much the tour people will refund, but I don't imagine it will be as much as I'd like. Besides, it most likely won't be for weeks, maybe months." A rueful little smile crossed her face. "What I have with me was to have been my spending money—you know, to buy a fisherman's knit sweater and some lace for my wedding dress, that kind of thing." She shot a glance at Michael Larkin. "The kind of thing all American tourists buy, I suppose."

"I see. Hmmm." Seamus took a sip of his tea, grudgingly pronounced it fine indeed, and added, "As you may have gathered, we need someone to help out for a bit. Would you consider stopping here with us? We can afford to pay you a fair wage, and you'd have a place as well. What do you say, girl?"

Brenna's eyes widened. "You're not serious?"

"I assure you he is, uh, Miss…" said Michael.

"Ryan, Brenna Ryan," she supplied coolly.

"He's quite serious. My father, as you no doubt see, is troubled with gout, and neither of us likes to miss a meal. I'm not so sure your staying is a good idea, however." Abruptly he stood, towering over her. "Please accept my apologies, Miss Ryan. My behavior, as you so colorfully put it, was reprehensible, but I hope you can find it in your heart to forgive me." He looked directly into her eyes and extended his hand.

"Of course," Brenna murmured, placing her hand in his. Her first thought was that he looked neither sorry nor eager for her forgiveness. But she was quickly dismayed by the unsettling effect of their brief moment of contact. It was Brenna who withdrew her hand from those slender, strong fingers she'd watched in the car, Brenna who looked away from his dark, uncompromising gaze.

"As I said, I'm not at all sure that what we need is an American tourist in our kitchen, but I bow to my father's judgment." The phrase *American tourist* carried all the connotations of *plague victim*. "And now, if you

16

will excuse me?" Without waiting for Brenna to reply, he sauntered from the room.

For a few moments the silence was profound. Brenna lowered herself into the chair Michael Larkin had vacated and turned to Seamus. "I really don't think your idea would work, Mr. Larkin. Thank you, but he...your son seems to have taken a dislike to me."

"Nonsense, girl. That's not it at all. Michael is just tired out. With my leg at the bum he's had to double up. Been going night and day and then some to keep apace. I want you to stay. I like a woman with spirit and you've got plenty, even if you are religious. Besides, you make a good sandwich," he added, glancing at the empty tray. "Like to cook?" She nodded, and Seamus, his gruff voice softened now, said, "Stay. We'll have a good time, girl, and you'll get a look at the Irish where they live. Isn't that what you want?" He even smiled at her.

"Yes, I guess it is." Brenna smiled back at the preposterous old man. How could he be so rude and bossy one minute and so...so endearing the next? "Who is Nola? Is she your son's wife?" She hardly knew where the words had come from.

But the old man just snorted. "Wife? Michael? No, no. She's the daughter of our housekeeper, Mrs. O'Malley, who's gone to be with her sister during her time. Now, Nola's a pretty little thing, for all her revolutionary ideas. But Michael's wife? No, I've a notion our Michael will never marry. You see, he's afraid of women."

Having no ready comment on this surprising statement, Brenna merely ignored it. "You're sure you wouldn't rather find a girl from the village?"

"The question is, are you sure you can put up with a crusty old man and a rude young one?" The twinkle in his eyes was unmistakable.

"I think I can manage. In fact," she responded

warmly to the outrageous old man, "I'm looking forward to it. I didn't want the average package tour in Ireland, and this is definitely far from it." She stuck out her hand, and he took it in his own. "A bargain, Mr. Larkin?"

"Seamus," he growled.

"Seamus it is. And now, I'd better start earning my keep." She picked up the tray and went along to the kitchen, the most extraordinary sense of well-being filling her despite the fact of Michael Larkin's rudeness.

Chapter Two

The morning sun was shining brightly, but the sun was not what had wakened Brenna. Nor was the strangeness of the second-floor room, charming though it was, the cause of her confusion as she struggled to come fully to her senses. The reason was a tiny, red-haired young woman, standing just inside the door with hands on shapely hips, brown eyes blazing.

"And who might you be?" Her voice thrummed with furious resentment. "And whatever are you doing in me own bed?" Brenna sat up then, and the covers fell away. "And you're wearin' my nightdress!"

Brenna's feet touched the floor and she stood uncertainly, looking down at the brief gown she wore. The gown was pale pink, liberally trimmed with white lace, and probably a perfect fit for a small, red-haired woman—like the indignant one who stood before her. "You must be Nola..."

"Aye, that I am! And who, may I ask, are *you*?"

All traces of sleep were gone now. With as much dignity as she could muster Brenna drew herself up to her full height, took the light coverlet from the bed, and wrapped it about her like a shawl. My name is Brenna Ryan, and I—" For a moment she faltered, then continued steadily. "I've been hired to help out for a while. Seamus—Mr. Larkin—said I could borrow your gown,

19

since my things are still in the village."

Nola ignored the reference to her gown for the moment. "That's ridiculous! Why would they hire someone? They've got me!"

"Whenever you choose to be here," said a voice from the door, which Nola had flung wide in her pique. Michael's eyes met Brenna's briefly. "Which is when it's convenient for you, Nola, not for us. Seamus asked Miss Ryan to help while your mother's away, and between them they made an agreement. You've been replaced."

Nola's answer was quick and profane. Brenna felt herself blush, thinking how Sam would tease her if he were there to see. But aloud she said calmly, "As soon as I get my things—" She broke off as she saw Michael reach down, pick up her two large bags and the smaller cosmetic case, and slide them into the room. "Oh, thank you, Mr. Larkin. It was good of you to get them."

He shrugged, glanced once more at her, and said dryly, "Seamus insisted. Otherwise you might catch cold...or get arrested." He turned, leaving her to cope with the still furious Nola.

"Look, Miss O'Malley, is it?" Nola gave an angry nod. "I came here sort of by mistake, but Seamus was good enough to invite me to stay. I want to, very much."

"I can imagine." Nola O'Malley jerked her head towards the hallway. "Well, it won't do you any good. That one's not available." She crossed to the small rocker on the other side of the bed and sat down. "So don't go getting any ideas."

Brenna pushed the door shut and hauled her bag onto the bed. Intent only on getting out of the other girl's clothes and into her own, she rummaged for something to wear. "I can assure you I'm not in the least interested in Michael Larkin."

"Then you're a walkin' corpse, luv," said Nola with a

low chuckle. "Women always make fools of themselves over men like Michael. They can't seem to help it."

Brenna dressed quickly, pulling on a lime green shirt-dress she found near the top of the bag. She brushed her black hair briskly with her head held down, then smoothed it into a wide gold barrette at the nape of her neck. Before she spoke, Brenna looked at Nola O'Malley, really looked at her for the first time. The girl's face was dominated by wide brown eyes and arching tawny brows. Her nose was small and straight, her mouth firm and well shaped, her complexion flawless. A lovely girl; and strangely enough, for it didn't happen often, a girl who roused in Brenna a sense of contrariness, of competition. She did not disguise her thorough examination, and neither did it seem to discomfit Nola. It was as though each recognized something worth considering in the other. Although the two generated a natural antipathy, strangely enough there existed a kind of wary respect between them as well.

Aloud Brenna said, "That may be true of other women, but not of me."

"Do you mean to say you aren't attracted to Michael Larkin?" Nola asked in disbelief.

After debating for an instant as to whether or not she should tell the truth to this outrageous girl, Brenna's basic honesty won out. "I didn't say he isn't attractive. I just don't intend to make a fool of myself."

Nola laughed, a low, pleasing sound. "That's easier said than done, ducks. Whether you fall for him or not, that remains to be seen. I wouldn't want to put the butter-and-egg money on it, though." She smiled, a malicious look in her bright eyes. "One thing's for certain, Michael's not likely to make a fool of himself over *you*."

Something in her tone made Brenna flare again with that uncharacteristic drive—competition. "You're sure of that, are you?"

"I'm sure. You're not his type. He hates American women. Says they're loud and pushy and wear too much makeup."

"I understand he's not too crazy about women, period," Brenna retorted, against her better judgment.

"It depends. I've never had trouble with any man, and I certainly wouldn't with Michael if I chose to have him, which I don't." She stood and sauntered insolently toward the taller girl. "You couldn't get him if you tried, though, I'd put money on that." The challenge was as plain as the pretty nose on her face. "Care to make a wager, dearie? Whatever they pay you for 'taking my place,' as *he* put it, you hand over to me if you can't get him to take a tumble. Well, luv?" she repeated, her brown eyes alight with amusement.

"I—" Brenna was trying to frame an appropriate reply when she heard Seamus bellow, his words clearly audible from below.

"Two females in the house, and not a sign of breakfast!"

She brushed past Nola. "Please excuse me, I've got to go fix breakfast."

"You do that, dearie, you do that. I like my sausages brown all round and my eggs done four minutes. Go it?" She chuckled at the look Brenna threw her as she left the room.

Downstairs Brenna found a thunder-faced Seamus leaning heavily on a dark, gnarled cane. "Now see here, girl, are you one of those slugabeds that doesn't get up until—" he sputtered, glaring at her.

"No, I usually get up fairly early, and I will from now on." She smiled, and was glad to see his face soften.

"Now, what can I fix you for breakfast?"

Mollified, he thought a minute, then ordered briskly, "Oats, sausage, muffins, and plenty of jam. And when you make the tea, make sure—"

"The kettle's at the boil!" she finished for him, laughing. Her laughter died away at the sight of Nola coming down the stairs. As she turned toward the kitchen she heard the banter begin between the old man and the girl. Although he was scolding her, the affection between them was obvious. She pushed open the door rather viciously, wondering why their conversation made her feel somehow left out. *Ridiculous!* She allowed herself one enormous sigh, however.

"Sounds as though you've got the weight of the world on your shoulders," said Michael, who emerged from the pantry at that moment. "Look, I suppose I could help you a bit 'til you find your bearings. The recipes are different, you know." His hands were full, and he proceeded to place several items on the table.

"That's all right," Brenna replied faintly, somewhat surprised by his attitude. "I don't use recipes much."

"Oh?" A quick look of concern crossed his face.

"Don't worry," she said, smiling. "I did once, but now I just sort of know how much of what goes in most things. My dad says I'm a pretty good cook, really."

"Good. For a moment you had me worried. I may be too busy to eat at times, but I enjoy good food. So if Seamus is set on having you here, and you're set on stopping, I can help you to find your way." He busied himself in the small, crammed refrigerator, bringing out a healthy string of fat sausages as well as butter, eggs, and a bottle of milk with the cream at the top. Laden once more, he made his way to the work area next to the stove. "You live with your father and mother, then?"

Encouraged by the casual, if not exactly friendly, interest in his tone, Brenna set about finding ingredients for muffins. As she peered at the oven controls she answered, "No, I live alone. My mother died when I was twelve, and my father remarried just last year."

"Some men don't know when they're well off," Michael muttered.

Brenna set the control of the oven at what she hoped was the correct temperature and straightened up, a frown creasing her brow. Michael Larkin's dark eyes seemed to be challenging her to refute his statement. The sausages in a large iron skillet began to sizzle slightly and released a savory smell into the cozy kitchen. Although she knew she should probably let his comment pass, somehow she couldn't resist. Slowly she measured out flour from the old tin on the drain board, glad to see that the salt was in plain sight in a small square wooden box labeled SALT. "Mr. Larkin, correct me if I'm wrong, but it sounds as though you're kind of soured on marriage."

"You are certainly not wrong," he answered shortly. "Marriage is a trap. If they last—and the odds against it are pretty high these days—two out of three ending up at the solicitor's in your own country, I believe—it only means some poor man's in the trap for life. A man's a fool to drive himself into a situation like that, especially if all he finds once he's there is misery." He stabbed a plump sausage a trifle viciously and managed to keep from wincing as the hot juices spattered on his arm.

She kept a straight face with effort. "What about a woman, then?"

He shot her scathing look. "Women are different.

24

They have marriage on their minds from the time they can talk. Care to deny that? I seem to remember your mentioning only last evening the lace for your wedding dress, I believe."

For a long moment Brenna did not answer, her concentration apparently focused on mixing the muffin batter just so. Then, she looked up and met his eyes squarely. "I wouldn't be telling the truth if I said I never thought of marriage. I've thought of it often." She ignored the look of cynical triumph that crossed his face. "But you may be surprised to know I don't worry about it."

"Why not? Have the poor fellow staked out already?"

"No, as a matter of fact I haven't met him yet," she answered firmly. "But I believe with all my heart that there is a man for me, and that God knows who he is."

Michael reached for a platter on the shelf to his left and began removing the sausages from the pan. "Don't tell me you believe that old saw about all marriages being made in heaven?"

"Not all marriages, but I can assure you mine will be." She gave him a bright smile and asked, "Now, can you tell me where the muffin tin is?"

He gestured towards a cupboard. "That would be a change. The marriages I've seen…" He stabbed the last sausage with a final vengeance. "You won't catch *me* near the altar."

Brenna whirled to deliver a sarcastic reply, but the door flew open and the elder Larkin came hobbling into the room. Seeing their joint efforts had resulted in his breakfast being nearly done, Seamus was exuberant. "There, I knew the two of you could get along!"

Luckily for all three, Michael's reply was lost in the flurry of activity and conversation Nola created as she swept into the room.

"What's this? Breakfast almost done and the table not set? No organization—" She bustled about, giving Brenna a welcome chance to subdue the unruly, contradictory feelings her conversation with Michael Larkin had created.

That afternoon Brenna had almost finished polishing the fine old furniture in the front room when she heard the lively sound of the door chimes. Dust cloth in hand, she started for the entry hall but saw Michael pass the arched doorway. Curious in spite of herself, she stood where she was and listened to Michael's conversation with the caller—a woman from the sound of the voice.

"Good day, Michael. Is Larkin in?"

"Yes, Molly, but he's lying down at present. His leg, you know. He won't always admit it, but he wants a good bit of rest. Could I possibly be of service?"

"Yes, Michael. It's Laddie. This morning he tried to jump the wall, as he always does, and well, see for yourself. I got him as far as the gate before he quit on me. The poor fellow can't put any weight a-tall on that back leg."

Curiosity got the better of Brenna, so she walked quietly to the open front door when the voices faded. There she saw Michael kneeling outside on the walk, examining a large, golden brown dog.

"Unless I miss my guess, Molly, it's a dislocated hip," he said.

The woman was also on her knees beside the injured dog, anxiously watching Michael. Brenna could only guess her age to be somewhere between fifty and sixty. Her hair was not gray, not red, but in the range of a coppery beige, and cut quite short. The riot of curls framed a warm and interesting face: large blue eyes, a nose slightly snubbed and tilted like a child's, and a generous mouth that was tight with concern now as she stroked the dog's head with a gentle hand.

"I can't abide seeing him in pain, Michael. Please, can you do something?" Her anguish was almost palpable.

"Yes, but I'll need someone to help me. It's definitely a job for two." He shook his head at her move to help. "No, no, Molly. I know it would hurt you worse than Laddie here, for he'll be anesthetized. I'll find someone."

"I'll be glad to help you." Brenna stepped forward. "Just tell me what to do."

"You?" Michael frowned, but before he could say anything more, Brenna went on.

"Yes, me. My father raised quarter horses, and I had my own horse from the time I was big enough to sit in a saddle. We always had animals around the place, and Dad said I was a pretty fair hand." She felt a little silly defending herself and was glad when Michael merely nodded.

"Right. We'll give it a try. Molly Fogarty, this is Brenna Ryan, who's, uh, helping out for a bit."

Molly smiled and nodded her head, but her attention was focused on the dog. Michael placed a hand on her arm. "You're welcome to wait, but it might be best if you just get home with you. I'll come to let you know as soon as I'm certain of his condition."

The older woman bit her lip, obviously torn, but after a moment she nodded. "Thank you, Michael. He's a good dog, you know...a good friend."

"I know, Molly, and I'll take good care of him." He gave her a quick hug, and she buried her curly head in his shoulder for an instant before she left, not looking back as she went through the gate. Then Michael turned his whole attention to the dog. "A nasty, painful thing to have happen to a poor creature is a dislocated hip." Gently he picked the animal up and carried him around the house, with Brenna close behind.

"What if you can't relocate it?" she asked.

He shook his head. "Not good. He'd form a false joint up higher, which would, of course, mean his leg would always be a little shorter. I'm glad she didn't wait to bring him in. Improves the chances."

Brenna hurried ahead to open the door he indicated with a nod of his head. She was surprised, considering the hominess of the rest of Crosswinds, to see what appeared to be a completely modern, fully equipped veterinary surgery. "What about the other dog, the one MacGill hit last night?"

"He belonged to the Rankins, just as MacGill thought. They came for him this mornin'. He'll be fine."

Carefully Michael slid Laddie onto the table and turned to face his assistant. "Now, there's a good measure of pulling involved. Are you up to it?"

"I'm sure." Brenna allowed herself to look briefly into his eyes and smiled. Somehow, here in his own professional surroundings he seemed different...more approachable.

"I do believe you are. OK, old Laddie, let's put you to sleep." He injected a needle into the trusting dog and released a clear fluid into the vein. The animal slowly relaxed until the full weight of his great head lay against Brenna's hand, his brown eyes closed in deep sleep. As Larkin took hold of the injured leg he instructed, "All you have to do is put your hands beneath his thigh and hold on. All right?" She nodded, determined to do the job whatever it took. She didn't want to examine her motives too closely, but she knew her determination had something to do with the way Michael Larkin felt about American tourists, and women in particular, and her wanting to prove him wrong.

Larkin was right about one thing. It was a difficult job. He pushed and pulled, trying without success for several long, anxious moments to manipulate the joint into precisely the right angle. Brenna watched his face intently, taking in the absolute concentration etched clearly on his features. With his strong jaw clenched, his dark eyes intent on the task before him, he was hardly aware of her at all, except as an ally in the struggle. It seemed a very long time before she heard a faint click and saw the relieved look on Michael's face.

"There, we've done it!" His jubilation was infectious, and Brenna shared in it fully.

"Will he be all right now? Is there a chance this will happen again?"

"Yes, as a matter of fact, there is. But I've the feeling Laddie here will be fine." He smiled, and the change in his lean, somber face was remarkable. "Thank you for your help. You were A-1."

Feeling a little light-headed at the unexpected praise, Brenna murmured something inane, thinking what a marvelous difference she felt when he smiled.

With great care Michael lifted the limp animal from the table and made him comfortable in one of the kennels on the far wall of the room. Then he straightened up, hands at the small of his back. "I could do with a cup of tea. And you?"

Not wanting to break the congenial mood, Brenna nodded. "I'll make it. Seamus has me trained fairly well already. I always make sure the—"

"—kettle's at the boil!" he rejoined as the two of them made their way to the kitchen, a truce of sorts in effect.

After a cup of tea that even Michael pronounced fine he pushed back his chair and stood. Brenna was sorry the peaceful little interlude was over, but gratified when he said casually, "I'd best go along and let Molly know Laddie is all right. Care to come with me, since you had a hand in his treatment? She only lives down the row."

"I'd love to." Brenna quickly stacked the teacups in the sink, laid a clean dish towel neatly over them and said, "There, let's go. I'll do those later."

But Larkin made no move to go as, a little frown on his face, he said, "I can't make up my mind whether you're efficient or lazy. It looks good," he waved a hand at the neat kitchen, "But Mrs. O'Malley would never leave a dirty dish...and neither did my mother."

A subtle change came over his face when he spoke of his mother; something that made Brenna uncomfortable without knowing why. "You sound as though being neither lazy nor efficient is commendable. How's a woman to win?"

He murmured something she didn't quite catch and headed for the door. She realized if she wanted to go she'd better get moving.

As Brenna and Michael sat in Molly Fogarty's wonderfully cluttered front room, she kept calling out to them from the kitchen, her voice bright with relief. She had insisted they take tea again.

"Michael will tell you, I've had Laddie since he was whelped. All the others in the litter died of distemper, and by some miracle the only one that made it was the runt, my Laddie!"

Quietly Michael said, "She fed him night and day with a dropper. Never saw anything like it."

"Mrs. Fogarty seems to be an unusual woman."

"It's Miss Fogarty. She's never married."

Brenna's eyes widened in surprise. "Really? She's so...so attractive, and this is such a marvelous house."

"Not what you'd expect a spinster's house to look

like, eh?" He followed her glance around the comfortable room with its deep rose-colored easy chairs, healthy green plants hanging in the windows, the full-to-overflowing bookshelves, with more magazines and books piled here and there, little collections of carved birds and animals, and lamps beside every available place so sit. Being an avid reader, Brenna noticed Molly's selection of books and liked the woman even more. "I love to come here," Michael continued, "always have. When I was a boy, I—"

"When you were a boy I couldn't keep you out of the cookie tin," said Molly as she brought in a tray laden with fragile, elegant white cups, a beautiful Staffordshire teapot, and a silver plate heaped high with cookies of several kinds.

"Well, it was always full, and Mother was keen on vegetables more than cookies, that's certain."

"Your mother was a good, sensible woman." Molly's voice was quiet and low.

She poured the tea and passed a cup to each, her face open and pleasant. Michael's face wore much the same expression. Yet Brenna sensed some undercurrent between the two. As Molly balanced her own delicate cup and saucer on her knee she said to Brenna, "I understand you elected to leave your tour group and stay on here at Clifden."

"Yes, I did." Brenna wondered for a moment how Molly had found out about her arrangement, then decided Clifden was probably like her own small home town. The same efficient method of passing interesting tidbits of information from one person to another would be in operation—gossip. She took a sip from her cup and remarked, "The tea here is so marvelous— really different from any we have at home. What is it?"

"Oh, it's probably much the same, only fresh, and

not in a paper bag." Molly gave a little shudder. "Those limp, soggy packets are abominable. I suppose people use them because they're less messy than leaves. But good tea is worth a little bother, I'd say. Now, won't you be missing some things you would have seen on the tour?"

"I'm sure I will. But somehow it seemed important to become acquainted with some of you, instead of being shown your houses from a bus and told about your history from a guide." She smiled. "You'll have to admit getting to know Seamus Larkin and meeting you and Laddie and learning how to make proper tea is a lot more appealing than a tour of a haunted castle, or a medieval banquet, or even kissing the Blarney stone!"

"I see what you mean. Seamus alone is worth more than a tour," Molly said wryly, "not to mention our Michael here. Have you heard the legend of the Blarney stone, by the way?"

Brenna shook her head, anticipating a good story.

"Well, it goes something like this. One day the king of Munster was enjoying a stroll by a lake on his vast property when he heard a voice crying for help. He was no coward, that man, and he jumped right into the lake and rescued a little bit of an old woman. Soon as she could speak she asked how she could repay him, and like the gentleman he was, he said her thanks were quite enough. But the poor man stuttered, and she told him there was something she could do for him, because she had fairy powers, she did. You're aware, no doubt, of the indisputable fact that there are wee fairies in Ireland?" She gave Brenna a mischievous grin.

Brenna glanced at Michael, who was watching Molly with such an affectionate, tender look in his eyes that she felt a pang of envy. "As a matter of fact, yes," she said, trying to keep her attention fully on Molly. "My dad was always saying something about the little folk when I was a kid. I believed every word!"

"Ah, yes. Well, the king believed, too, and when he admitted he should like to be more eloquent, that little old woman fixed her eyes on the topmost tower of his castle, whispered several Gaelic phrases, then told the king to climb to the top, lean out the window, and kiss the stone below. She called it the Blarney stone. Well, the king wanted to stop that infernal stuttering so he did as he was told. From that day on, he had the gift of a silver tongue and never stammered again. He became known for his elegant, beautiful language. Being a good and generous king, he thought it a good thing to share the marvelous gift and welcomed all his subjects to come and kiss the Blarney stone themselves. From that day to this, the Blarney stone has been a symbol of eloquent speech. And it's no easy feat to kiss it," she said with a twinkle in her eye, "although the tourists manage it by the score. I've done it meself."

"That's a great story," responded Brenna. "You sound as though you've told it more than once."

"She certainly has. Our Molly was once a tour guide herself," put in Michael. "Why, I've heard she was so silver-tongued and eloquent, not to mention the prettiest girl guide they ever had, that they were after her for years to come back after she up and quit her job."

"Oh, Michael, go on with you!" Molly said, but Brenna could tell she was pleased. "Now tell me more about Laddie, and what I must do to make certain he recovers."

While the two of them plunged into the details of Laddie's condition and treatment, Brenna observed them both more closely. Their easy camaraderie was very appealing. When Molly left a few minutes later to replenish the cookie platter, Brenna said softly to Michael, "You two seem to get along so well—and it's not just the cookies, either."

He nodded and made a surprising reply. "If things had been different, she could have been my mother."

Once again Brenna was aware of things unsaid, stories untold. Molly came back into the room, bringing with her that indefinable, marvelous energy that seemed to be both soothing and stimulating. *A totally fascinating lady*, Brenna decided. One last impression lodged itself in her consciousness when, just before they left, Brenna caught a glimpse of a worn Bible on Molly's bedside table with a pair of old-fashioned, round spectacles on top. The lace scarf beneath and an old satin glass lamp beside made the scenario look like a clever decorator's touch. But somehow Brenna knew the Book was one with which Molly Fogarty was intimately acquainted.

Chapter Three

When Brenna opened her eyes the next morning Nola's room was still strange and unfamiliar, giving an unreal quality to what had passed the previous day. The sloping ceiling, pierced by a dormer window, faced the high, four-postered bed where she sat. A small, red velvet upholstered window seat looked as though it had seen much use, but there was very little other furniture. A wicker rocking chair with a wild print chintz cushion, a square oak table beside it, and a tall armoire of some dark, carved wood crowded the walls. She woke sufficiently to remember that she was still in County Galway, Ireland, in Clifden-by-the-Sea! The realization filled her with a quick excitement, and she slipped from the tumbled bed to the window seat, her feet tucked beneath her as she gazed out the window.

The rooftops, some slate, some thatch, sat protectively atop the homes of Clifden, guarding against the creeping wraiths of early morning mist. She breathed a sigh of pure contentment and bowed her head in a prayer of thankfulness.

Oh, Lord, how wonderful it is to be here. Help me to make the most of this day....

At last she stirred, telling herself Seamus would be growling if she wasn't down soon. She chose a pale cream sweater that, as Leslie had often said, fit her just right. A sleek denim skirt and low-heeled shoes completed her outfit. After all, she was a housekeeper now. A giggle rose to her lips as the thought struck her; somehow, Leslie's hooting laughter sounded in her mind. "A housekeeper! Honestly, Brenna," she would probably say, "you are *strange*, you know that?"

Maybe so, she thought as she rummaged for an apron in the big, cheery kitchen. *Maybe so*. But somehow, it suited her to be right exactly where she was, doing exactly the thing she was doing now: whisking eggs to a foamy froth for omelets. Uncertain whether the two men liked omelets, she decided to fix them anyway because she did them well. She diced potatoes and chopped onion and cheese with a paring knife, for there was no grater to be found.

When, as though drawn by the aroma of sizzling onions, the two men appeared, Brenna looked up and smiled brightly. "Top of the mornin' to you!"

Seamus growled. "You'll not be hearing a real Irishman say that. By the Lord Harry, that's just for tourists."

Brenna refused to be baited. "And what do you think I am, sir?"

"Well, with a name like Brenna Ryan, if you'd hold your tongue you might be taken for an Irish lassie. You do have some Irish in you somewhere, I trust," he said, maneuvering his game leg into a chair.

She nodded. "My father named me Brenna because he said it meant 'maiden with raven tresses.' They tell me I had plenty of black hair even when I was born." She smiled as she thought of John Ryan. "He always wanted to come to Ireland, but somehow he never got the opportunity."

"So you came instead," said Seamus.

"Something like that. Now, have your breakfast. Or do you prefer to eat in the dining room?" She stopped, pan in mid-air, flipped the omelet deftly, folded it, then slid the puffy golden triangle smoothly onto a warm plate. "On second thought, sit in here, it'd be more convenient for me."

Seamus's face registered surprise, but Michael, who'd not spoken until now, could not quite suppress a slight smile. "She's right, Seamus. It smells delightful, Miss Ryan."

"I'll serve your father first, if that's all right."

Michael nodded, and neither man spoke again until they'd finished eating. It was Seamus who said, "That was excellent, girl, excellent. I must confess I've never had taties in my eggs just that way. And for an Irishman to have to confess he's not had them in every way there is, must be somethin' like saying 'Top o' the mornin'— just not the way a real Irishman conducts himself." His brows lowered as he added, "Our Nola has taken herself off again, so you're on your own as to the cooking."

As Brenna cleared away the table she was far from displeased at this news. And later, faced with the prospect of preparing dinner, she was glad to find a fine pork loin in the icebox. Seamus was napping and Michael had gone out, so she determined to make a presentable meal with whatever she found on hand. The notion of a table garden was in the back of her mind, and when she stepped out the kitchen door, sure enough, there was a pocket-sized square of neat rows. A line of bricks separated a narrow strip on two sides, and to her delight she found basil, parsley, garlic, and some other plants she didn't readily recognize. Her experience with fresh herbs was not extensive because of the demands on her time that her job made, but she loved experimenting, and happily plucked and snipped and cut in the well-cared-for little garden.

The tattered cookbook she found tucked in back of

the castor sugar was evidently one of Mrs. O'Malley's favorites, because dinner—which when finally done consisted of roast pork with herbs, fried potatoes, broad beans, and apricot souffle—was an unqualified success. Even Nola, back for the meal and extremely quiet for a change, seemed to enjoy it.

Seamus put his hands on his broad belly and gave a contented sigh. "Girl, that was as fine a meal as I've eaten. That apricot concoction quite fine, quite fine."

"Pretty simple, really," said Brenna. "I just looked to see what there was in the refrigerator, found apricot jam and eggs. Then I looked for a recipe to go with them."

"Thought you never used recipes," said Michael with a sidelong glance.

"Oh," answered Brenna, a little disturbed by the light sarcasm in his tone, "I didn't say I never did. Usually it's when I'm not sure of something, or—" She wanted to add, *Or I'm not sure of someone's reactions, like yours, Michael Larkin*; but she didn't. Instead she found a little smile and went on, "—or when I have ingredients I'm not familiar with, like the herbs."

Nola, surprisingly silent until this juncture, spoke up. "Me mum won't like it when she finds you've been mucking about in her garden."

"Nonsense," said Seamus. "You know as well as I that a garden wants regular using. Of course you realize if you use it you must weed it as well, my girl," he added with a malicious twinkle at Brenna. "All the same, the joint was delicious, wasn't it, Michael?"

Almost grudgingly Michael said, "As matter of fact it was very good. Let's see, it had garlic, parsley, onion, and—" He looked at her, his expression pretty well devoid of animosity for once, and she couldn't help but respond.

"There was fresh basil, and lemon rind," she supplied. "The recipe said the meat should be marinated overnight, but of course there wasn't time. I…I enjoy cooking," she finished quietly, a little disconcerted by his steady, penetrating gaze.

"Well, it was a fair meal, I'll grant you that, but there's more important matters to discuss," said Nola. "Unless, of course, you're nothing but a woman who's looking for a man and is using food for bait." She glanced slyly at first Michael and then Brenna. But Brenna was calmly finishing her dessert.

Seamus gave a snort. "Speakin' of bein' after a man, Nola, have you hogtied that young assassin you've been a-chasin' these many months?" Like Brenna, there were times that Seamus slipped into a broader accent; perhaps he knew it or perhaps it was unconscious. At any rate, his words inflamed Nola.

"He's not an assassin!" she denied hotly. "Just because a man has strong convictions and is willing to take action is no reason to speak ill of him!"

Michael leaned back in his chair, a watchful look in his eyes. "He was involved in that bombing last month in Belfast, was he not? In the LaMon House Hotel, where they dug out twelve bodies that have not all been identified even yet?"

"That's not been proved, Michael Larkin, and I'll thank ye not to spread the nasty rumor of it!" Nola said, her voice shaking with anger. "At least someone is doing something, whether or no it is Sean. Not like some, who choose to ignore the situation."

Her words were plainly accusing, but Michael merely shrugged. "I don't believe violence is the answer. Ireland has had enough violence to last forever." He turned from Nola to Brenna. "I'm surprised you came to our country for a holiday. Surely your newspapers

39

must carry ghastly stories of the bombings, the riots...weren't you afraid to come?"

"I was, a little," Brenna admitted. "But we were also told that 'the Trouble,' I believe you call it, was not everywhere in Ireland."

"It is that—everywhere, believe me," muttered Seamus.

"Oh," Brenna hastened to add, "I didn't mean you don't feel the pain of a divided country, Seamus, really I didn't. I meant the fighting, the bombs and guns. We've been told it is mostly confined to Northern Ireland. We didn't plan to go there," she finished quietly.

"And you'd best not," said Nola. "Stay here, where it's quiet and idyllic, and safe, and there's no danger. Lots of fine Irishmen do it, why not you?" She got up from the table abruptly, daring Michael to defend himself.

He merely said, "I refuse to let you goad me into fighting, verbally or otherwise, Nola."

"Because you're a coward!"

"Silence!" thundered Seamus. "Because you and your friends have chosen violent revolution as a way of life there's little hope for peaceful revolution and change. I agree with Michael."

Michael did not acknowledge his father's defense as he softly said, "It is not those who can inflict the most, but those who can suffer the most, who will conquer."

"Bah! What do *you* suffer, here in this forsaken village with your comfortable life, and where did that fine philosophy get the fine Terence MacSwiney who said it?" For a moment Nola stood, hands on hips, head proudly tilted as she glared at the three of them. Then with one last angry retort she left the room like a small, red-haired whirlwind. "I'll not be botherin' you fine patriots for a spell; my country calls!"

For a moment or two after she was gone they all were silent, each thinking that if you didn't agree with Nola O'Malley, she *was* a fine spectacle to behold in her fervor. Brenna rose to clear the table, and when she was finished she broke the silence with a hesitant question. "Who was Terence MacSwiney?"

"A poet, a man with convictions stronger than Nola's," answered Seamus. "He died for them."

"How? Was he killed?"

"No," said Michael grimly. "Hunger strike."

"Oh," said Brenna, her voice small, "I see. I also see I read the wrong books about Ireland before I came."

"No history, I suppose?" Michael's look was cynical again. "I understand Americans are only big on their own history, and biased against the British at that. At least we have something in common."

"No, I didn't read enough about Irish history," Brenna admitted. "But I'd like to learn." She was trying to respond quietly, when sarcasm was on the tip of her tongue. *A soft answer turneth away wrath* flitted through her mind, and she thought of the plaque in the hall at home, emblazoned with hand-painted sunflowers and that very motto. Her mother had hung it there, many years before she died. *A soft answer*. "Do you have any books I can read?"

The cynicism faded from Michael's expression and a grudging respect took its place as he said, "A few. But with Seamus about, you don't need books. He's a walking book himself where Ireland's concerned. Tell her how it all began, Daddy."

The use of the simple homely term by Michael for his father caught Brenna unaware. A lump formed in her throat; beneath the rude, brusque surface of the man was a tender heart, she knew now for sure. She cleared her throat and tried to sound casual. "I'd love to find out more about your country's history, Seamus."

A pleased, gratified look spread over the old man's face, and Michael said drily, "You'll excuse me, while I go and make a fresh pot of tea during the history lesson. Once you start him he may go on into the night."

Seamus's face now wore the familiar scowl. "Go on with you, Michael, we don't need you. Sure, girl, I'd not be talking *all* the night, but it's a sad tale, and I'm not certain where to begin...."

"Begin with the coming of the Celts, Seamus. Then you'll only have fourteen or fifteen hundred years to go," said Michael as he sauntered from the room.

"There's no need for sarcasm, my boy," said Seamus aggrievedly. He gave a great sigh as he rose from the table and made his painful way over to the favored plush chair. As unobtrusively as possible Brenna helped him get settled and put a soft knitted blanket of fine blue wool over his legs. "Thank ye, girl. You're not a bad lassie." A roguish look came into his eyes, "For an American tourist, at least."

"You're bound and determined not to let me live that down, aren't you?" She grinned good-naturedly and asked, "Is there a time you can pinpoint when it began? The Trouble, I mean."

"That's a hard question, but you can be sure it has to do with *them*." The look on his face was grim. "In the first place, being an island means Ireland must be sought out. For instance, as you did. And why did you come here, girl?"

Caught unaware by the sudden piercing question, Brenna bit her lip, a frown creasing her brow. Finally she said slowly, "Partly because my father's parents were born here long ago, and partly because of the things I read: the feeling of time arrested, of a fascinating people who laugh and are fiercely proud." She ducked her head, then looked up. "It sounds foolish and romantic when I say it out loud, but it's true. I've mooned over pictures of Ireland and books about Ireland as long as I can remember. The stories about the courage and beauty of the Irish as a people have been part of my whole life, my Dad saw to that. There just wasn't any other place that came close when I had saved enough money to take a trip. I...I guess I came to see if it was like my dreams about it."

He nodded. "Many others have also come, though for far less harmless reasons than yours. For instance the Celts were first, then around the eighth century came the Danes. Some folks swear that's where all the red-headed Irishmen sprung from."

Against her will Brenna thought of Michael, who was still in the kitchen. "What about those with dark hair and eyes, the ones I suppose everyone calls the *black Irish*?"

Seamus chuckled and gave her a sly glance. "Well, I'm not for certain, but the lassies think it a winning combination. And you, girl?"

Embarrassed that she had brought it up, Brenna merely said, "Go on with the history lesson, sir."

He grinned but challenged her no further. "In the twelfth century Henry II of Britain was 'given' Ireland in a papal bull. Hear you that?"

"What do you mean, *given*?"

"Oh, t'was to be his inheritance. They surely never consulted the Irish people, did they *wish* to be a gift!"

"It became a legal thing, then?" asked Brenna thoughtfully.

"More or less, and a heap sight less than more. T'was trickery, plain and simple."

"That's terrible!"

"To be sure, but not as bad as the fighting that followed. The king sent Strongbow the Norman, who beat out the Celts, and then he 'claimed' Ireland for the crown. They drove out the Danes and the Normans went about making themselves more Irish then the Irish." His face wore a scowl of mammoth proportions, as though he thought such an undertaking an impossibility, and a ridiculous one at that.

"Then the British have ruled over Ireland for—"

"Ruled? Never! They have oppressed us, taxed us unfairly, imposed inhuman penal laws, denied us the most basic rights that every free-breathin' man on God's green earth is entitled to. In short, in one way or another they have done their best to bleed us dry, but they have *never ruled us*!"

Sensing that she was being less than prudent but wanting to divert the old man's anger, Brenna said, "The Irishmen I've heard about are anything but dry, sir."

Before he could reply Michael came in with a tea tray. "If you're referring to alcoholic spirits, that's true of more than is good for us. Wasn't it George Bernard Shaw who said the Irishman finds his imagination too tortuous to bear without whiskey?" He set the tray down on the low table beside his father and busied himself with pouring, making Brenna think that he and Seamus must have done a great deal of shifting for themselves in one way or another. "I'm a teetotaller myself; 'tis simply a complication I cannot abide. Now if you were speaking of wit, and not spirits, I find a great many of my countrymen quite dry, and you'll not find their equal as storytellers, I'll wager."

Brenna took the steaming cup he offered and met his eyes with a smile. "I stand corrected. It seems I don't know enough Irishmen well enough. But I'd like to...."
Her voice trailed off and she wondered if he would

place the wrong meaning on her words. However, Michael merely turned to serve his father, making sure the milk and sugar were exactly to the old man's liking.

Seamus shook his shaggy head, a remote look on his face. "It was the famine, the failure of the spuds that was almost our undoing, girl. Have you any idea how many died?"

"No, I'm afraid I don't."

Soberly he said, "A million at least, maybe more."

Brenna slipped her shoes off and tucked her feet beneath her; she suppressed a little shudder. "*That* many? How long did it go on, anyway?"

"It was from 1845 to 1850 that the thing raged," Michael said grimly. "The ones who stayed in Ireland died of starvation and the ones who fled died of horrible conditions on board the ships. Floating coffins, they were called."

"And all the while the absentee landlords, who had their own fancy debts to pay, foreclosed right and left, and took the wee farms, leveling the poor cottages and leaving the people homeless as well as starving!" The intensity of Seamus's words made Brenna fear for his blood pressure, but she kept silent.

His eyes faraway and brooding, Michael said, "The terrible irony of the whole situation is the fact that there was enough and plenty of food to feed the starving of Ireland, but the landlords went about business as usual, shipping the cattle and crops off to England."

"But why?" she said, perplexed. "Weren't the people here, in a sense, English citizens?"

"In a sense, in a pig's eye!" Seamus snorted. "Only in the case when we could be useful to the British did they ever consider us 'English', and I for one was born an Irishman and will die an Irishman! They have never had respect for us. Most Britons consider us a drunken, no-good lot, best ruled with a foot on our necks!"

Michael did make an effort to soothe the old man then. "Here, now, Daddy, calm yourself. There's nothing to be gained by railing over it—"

"And not much by bombing and fighting, so where's the answer?" thundered Seamus. "It's been brother against brother, the Catholic against the Protestant. No peace, no peace."

All three were quiet for several moments, thinking their own thoughts. Brenna knew within reason that hers were far different from those of either of the two men, and the quiet warmth of the pleasant room almost lulled her into keeping silent. But something deep within her, a strong urge to speak what she knew without question to be the truth, made her say, "It seems to me that there's been nothing said of—" She stopped, aware of the intent, almost hostile look on Michael's face.

"What, girl?" prompted Seamus. "Speak up."

"Yes, tell us if you have the answer," said Michael, his tone plainly indicating he thought this highly unlikely, considering the longstanding complexity of the situation.

With an effort Brenna kept her voice steady as she said, "There's been no mention of God, only religion. And the two are far from the same, especially now. I...I just feel if there was a *real* Christian spirit present, much of the suffering and agony would be—"

Michael interrupted coldly. "You're like most people who know a little about a situation. You think the answers are simple, if only the stupid people involved would wake up and see them. You're wrong, as most are. You don't have the solution."

"But He is, Christ *is* the solution!"

For answer Michael stood and began stacking the tea

things onto the tray, then strode angrily from the room.

Stunned, Brenna stared after him. Surprisingly it was Seamus, who said, kindness in his gruff tone, "There, there, my girl, he's got a heap of bitterness in him. Don't think it's all directed at you, 'tisn't. Other things besides the Trouble stack up on him. His mum was—" He stopped, a closed, gloomy expression settling on his craggy old face.

She rose slowly. "I'll go and tend to the dishes. Thank you for the history lesson, Seamus." He only nodded broodingly, and when she got to the kitchen Michael was curt in his refusal to allow her to help. After watching him for a few moments as he, back turned, efficiently dispatched the dishes from sudsy water to drainboard, she finally turned and made her way up to her room, feeling very lonely indeed.

Chapter Four

Brenna walked briskly toward Sky Road, mentally checking off her purchases. A fine beefsteak, some wonderful cheese, six comice pears and some apples, bread (she'd admitted ruefully to Seamus that bread-making, except biscuits and cornbread, was beyond her experience), and eight skeins of the most beautiful creamy wool she'd ever seen. A small smile curved her mouth. She couldn't knit, but Molly had promised to give her instructions, and the lady at Millar's Wool Shop had waved her hands as though it was nothing at all to whip up a sweater in a week or two.

The smile faded from her face as she thought with a pang that several days of her time here were gone already. She switched the heavy string shopping bag from one arm to the other, glad the Larkin house wasn't far now. *Crosswinds*. Even the name pleased her. She ran over the list of things yet to do before lunch, and almost laughed out loud as she realized she was working quite hard for her bed and board, which Michael had given so reluctantly.

Michael. His dark eyes and dour expression flashed into her mind; the unhappy ending to last night's dinner still troubled her. He'd had only his tea that morning, saying as he left there was no time for breakfast, that O'Brian's prize bull was ailing. Brenna suspected

48

he could have taken the time to eat but didn't because of her presence. So she said nothing; only fixed breakfast for a glum Seamus, who seemed off his feed a little. She sighed, wondering if the whole idea of her staying in the Larkin household had been wise after all. But not being a woman who backs out of an agreement, she lifted her chin when she saw Michael's blue Austin in the drive and marched up the path.

He was there, all right, in the front room with a mighty scowl on his face, sitting at the secretary with an untidy pile of papers.

"Hi," said Brenna, determined to be cheerful. "I've been to town, or to the village, or whatever you call it."

He glanced up, his expression unchanged. "I'm having the devil of a time with these statements and would appreciate a pot of tea."

Steeling herself against the brusqueness in his tone, she said, "Have you eaten lunch yet?" He shook his head, shuffling again through a stack of papers. There was no use waiting for him to say anything more; she knew he wouldn't. In silent exasperation she navigated her way through the swinging kitchen door and laid her armload of purchases on the old pine table. As always when several tasks confronted her, she named them in her mind and shuffled them in order of importance: set the kettle on to boil, put away the vegetables, fruit, butter, and meat, and make a quick sandwich for the surly son of the house.

Always able to work and think quite well at the same time—unlike her brother Sam, who had the reputation of being unable to chew gum and walk—Brenna put the finishing touches on an appealing lunch tray. Two hearty beef sandwiches, a pear, a pot of tea, and a slice of the cake she'd baked that morning before going shopping. Her thoughts were not as pleasant as the tray.

She kept making up and revising dialogues with Michael Larkin, most of which were very much along the lines of telling him he was a rude, ill-tempered bully and that he needed very badly to grow up.

"*Where's my tea?*"

His voice from down the hall sounded remarkably like Seamus. Her teeth set, Brenna picked up the tray and marched in, found a real smile, and said, "That looks like a week's work."

At the fresh scent of the tea she was pouring he looked up. "That, or more, and I've only about another half hour until I must leave for a call." He took a grateful sip of the tea, then hunched again over the column of figures in the ledger.

"I could help." The words were out before she thought.

Michael looked up again. "No, no. Wouldn't think of it." Seeing the sandwiches, he reached for one with his left hand, a sheaf of papers in his right.

There was silence for a few moments as he wrote and munched and scowled simultaneously. Finally she ventured, "But why not? After all, I work with figures every day, and my boss seems to think I'm capable." Inwardly she fumed; why did she always wind up defending herself to this exasperating man?

"I'm certain you're quite capable, Miss Ryan. However, Seamus and I have always found we were equal to the task."

"But that was when Seamus was well, wasn't it? Really, Mr. Larkin, you're one of the most—" He looked up at her, his dark eyes filled with something she couldn't quite put a name to. It wasn't merely antagonism or pride, though they were present; in the long moment that passed she thought perhaps she saw a dare that she respond in kind to his rudeness, and perhaps a note of appeal so faint she was not at all certain of it. Before she could think of an appropriate reply, however, he spoke again.

"You're doing too much already. You cook, clean, do the marketing, the washing up—too much!"

Brenna took her cue from his words. "In the first place," she said pleasantly, "this is a wonderful old house and I love puttering around in it, especially after the pace in my office the past few months. Do you have any idea of how much work selling a pipeline to a group of Japanese oilmen involves? But I understand your position. You don't like being beholden to anyone."

He leaned his head to one side and propped it up with his hand, the fingers covering his brow as though it ached. "Do I dare ask under what category a word like *beholden* comes under? A Southern colloquialism, no doubt?"

A little of the tension had gone out of the air and Brenna felt herself relax as she nodded. "It means…oh, that you don't want to owe something to someone."

"I thought so. And you're right, I don't." His intense gaze failed to stop Brenna.

"Well, why don't I do what I can with the books while you're gone on your call, and then I'll tell you what payment I feel the job is worth?"

"You'll do that?" The relief he felt at seeing a way out of the onerous job before him was so obvious it was almost comical. "We'll make it a business arrangement, right?"

"Right," she assured him. "I really don't think it would be wise to trouble Seamus with it."

"He's the one who usually keeps things straight, although I'll have to admit he's no more a hand at it than I am. He's just more patient."

"Have you looked in on him today?"

"No, he was asleep when I came in. Why?" There was a note of anxiety in his voice.

"Oh, I'm not sure, but I thought he had a temperature. He wouldn't let me check it. I felt of his forehead, though," she added defiantly, "and he seemed warm."

"Maybe I'd better go up…" But the telltale glance at his watch was revealing.

"You have an appointment soon, don't you?"

"Yes, but—"

"Go on, and I promise to look in on him very soon." She made a wry little face. "That is, if he doesn't beat me to it and ring that blasted bell again." At the questioning look on his face she explained, "I found a little silver bell in the china cabinet and told him to ring if he wanted anything. He took me seriously and has been using it liberally."

Michael allowed himself a chuckle. "The old rascal, he's wrapped you 'round his finger." He gave one of the untidy stacks of papers a last ineffectual shuffle and rose from the desk, but he paused at the door, sandwich in one hand, pear and cake in the other. "It stills seems as though both of us are taking advantage of you."

Brenna gave him a long, level look, then smiled. "Mr. Larkin, don't worry about a thing. You're going to pay well for my services."

He returned her smile, but there was a rueful look on his face. "I'm beginning to wonder if you're not more clever than I reckoned."

"Now that could very well be." She slipped into his chair and bent her head to the tangled mess on the desk, not even looking up until she heard the front door close.

It was almost an hour before she heard the vigorous tinkling of the silver bell from Seamus's upstairs bedroom. She straightened and pressed both hands to the small of her aching back. The chaos on the desk was much better; the ledger wasn't current, but she had made immense progress. Michael had neglected to mention that Seamus had, before his illness, obviously been fairly prompt in his posting, if not overly neat. She had only to follow his example, for he had been interrupted as far as she could determine sometime around the middle of the preceding month. The bell rang again, even more imperiously, and she glanced at the clock. One-fifteen.

As she buttered bread and took out the wonderfully fragrant hunk of cheese she'd bought earlier, she thought again how extraordinary it was that she was so content in this place so very far away from home, and how easily she'd slipped into the pattern of living with these two men.

An hour later Brenna had to admit that Molly's unexpected visit probably was more responsible for Seamus's improved spirits than her lunch. She watched in amusement as the two of them teased each other unmercifully. Molly's blue eyes were snapping now as she said, "Well, if you're going to get insulting, Seamus Larkin, I'll take meself on home." As if to make good her threat she rose from her chair.

Seamus's bushy brows quirked in real alarm, though he tried to hide it. "Now, now, Molly, ye allus were a poor sport."

"Me? You old rascal, I've a notion not to tell you I've a pot of lamb stew simmerin' and I'd planned to invite you all to sup with me." With her hands on her hips she put Brenna in mind of Nola, except there was a softness, a gentleness about Molly that Nola would never have.

"Now, now," soothed Seamus. "This poor child

Brenna here has been laboring all day, and she deserves a respite. You wouldn't want to deny her that, would you?"

Molly pretended to deliberate a moment, then said to Brenna, "How about it, would you like for me to bring my pot over here, lass?"

"I'd love it! Seamus wasn't joking when he said I'd been busy. There's nothing started for dinner, and besides, I'd like more visiting with you," she finished. She usually took her time making friends; quite often it was the other person, like Leslie, who made the first overtures of friendship, and even kept it going. But with Molly she had felt quite at home from the beginning.

"How'd you like to learn to make soda bread?" asked Molly.

"I certainly would, but is it difficult?"

"No, not at all. I'll show you."

Plaintively Seamus spoke up. "What about me? Are both you women going to leave me all alone, and me feeling so poorly?"

"Ah, you'll just be wantin' sympathy," said Molly, but Brenna saw the look of affection in her eyes as she laid a hand on his cheek. "You're warm, Seamus."

"Poppycock! Women…always hovering and mucking about." He scowled, then said, "Well, how about reading a bit at least, before you desert me."

"I'll read if you'll let Brenna take your temperature," Molly said with a challenging little look.

"Absolutely not! I don't have a fever."

"Then we'll see you tomorrow." Molly took Brenna's arm and began to walk toward the door.

"All right, all right," said Seamus, giving in most ungraciously to what they all knew was necessary blackmail. "The Yeats is on the dresser."

"I know where the Yeats is, Seamus. I can also recite

by heart the ones you'll want, I'll wager."

He shrugged and allowed Brenna to place the thermometer in his mouth, then struggled to speak around it. "But I might want—"

"Hush." Molly retrieved the slim, leather-covered volume and settled comfortably in the deep wing chair by Seamus's bed.

Before she could begin, however, he defiantly plucked the offending thermometer out and said, "Read the one where the marker is first." He then popped it back in, arms crossed on his broad chest, knowing he'd won.

Molly shook her head in exasperation but did as she was bidden. Her voice was low and melodious, and, as she read the poem, Brenna leaned against the wall on the far side of the room, mesmerized.

All things uncomely and broken, all things worn
   out and old,
The cry of a child by the roadway, the creak of a
   lumbering cart,
The heavy steps of the ploughman, splashing in the
   wintry mould,
Are wronging your image that blossoms a rose in
   the deeps of my heart.

The wrong of unshapely things is a wrong too
   great to be told;
I hunger to build them anew and sit on a green
   knoll apart,
With the earth and the sky and the water, remade,
   like a casket of gold
For my dreams of your image that blossoms a rose
   in the deeps of my heart.

There was a small silence when she stopped; in spite

of the thermometer in his mouth Seamus did not look foolish. His expression was softer than Brenna had ever seen it, and though he did not look at Molly it was clear that his thoughts were of her. His gaze was on the open window, with its calm green view of the leafy upper branches of the beech tree that grew beside the house. Feeling like an intruder, Brenna crossed the room quietly and took the thermometer from his mouth, feeling a stab of concern as she read more than 101 degrees.

"You go ahead and read some more, Molly, and I'll be downstairs if you need anything." She left, feeling as though she had witnessed a very private moment. Outside the room she heard Seamus's gruff voice, but it was different than she'd ever head before.

"I want to give you that book, Molly."

"But Seamus, I know how you love it—"

"That's why I want you to have it. And at the risk of seeming an old fool...." He was quiet for a moment, and Brenna told herself she should go downstairs, for she was quite aware she was eavesdropping. But she stayed rooted while Seamus, his voice low, began,

> When you are old and gray and full of sleep,
> And nodding by the fire, take down this book,
> And slowly read, and dream of the soft look
> Your eyes had once, and of their shadows deep;
>
> How many loved your moments of glad grace,
> And loved your beauty with love false or true;
> But one man loved the pilgrim soul in you,
> And loved the sorrow of your changing face;
>
> And bending down beside the glowing bars,
> Murmur, a little sadly, how Love fled
> And paced upon the mountains overhead
> And hid his face amid a crowd of stars.

As Brenna stole down the stairs, the words *a crowd*

of stars danced through her head. A lovely poem, and the two upstairs were, or could have been, a lovely pair. She wondered what lay behind the strong, deep friendship that was so obvious now.

With no dinner to begin, she made herself a cup of tea. As she waited for the water to boil her mind wandered, and she wondered where Michael was and when he'd return. She gathered up what looked to be someone's favorite dog-eared Agatha Christie—but one she hadn't read—a box of stationery and a pen, and went outside to the little kitchen garden.

But she didn't write, nor did she read. She soon found, to her delight, that the walled garden beyond the area Mrs. O'Malley tended so carefully had been allowed to grow as it would. It had been well planned originally, with brick walks laid out in a precise herringbone pattern. The late spring growth of lilacs and lavender were fading, but roses and stock were in lush profusion now. In the far corner she found a tiny gazebo that had been planted long ago with vines of some sort, now grown lush and wild. The green shelter was furnished simply with a pair of high-backed wicker chairs facing each other, and she curled up to read in one, finding its faded blue cushions deep and soft. The book slipped, forgotten, to the floor as she allowed herself a daydream in which Michael humbly thanked her for setting his life, as well as his accounts, aright. With a chuckle at the unlikelihood of this occurrence, she took the pen and a sheet of pale blue stationery and wrote out a fanciful little statement of her charges for straightening out his account book.

After a while she stretched, laid the pen and paper on the stone floor, eased her head back and closed her eyes, giving her senses totally to the lovely soft summer sounds and smells all around her. The bees were out in force, and soon their drone became a part of her curious half-awake, half-asleep state; the scent of grass and flowers and early summer lulled her away.

She woke to find Michael Larkin in the chair opposite her and thought she must still be dreaming. She opened her mouth to speak, but when she saw that he was asleep, she was quiet. He looked so vulnerable… younger, somehow. His lashes, as they are so often on small boys, were very thick and dark against his cheek. There was no hint of sarcasm or antagonism in his face now, and she felt a treacherous tightness in her throat as she gazed at him, unable to look away. His mouth was well shaped, relaxed now in the merest hint of a smile. She wondered what made him the way he was, what had caused the wary sharpness in him.

When he opened his eyes she was staring right into them. "Been watching me sleep?" he asked with a long lazy stretch.

"Why, I…" Brenna stammered; it suddenly seemed an unbearably intimate thing for her to do.

His face showed amusement. "It's all right, really, because I watched you for a while."

"You did?" Before she could think, her hands flew to her hair and she unclasped the barrette nervously.

"Um hum. Don't worry, you look all right."

At his matter-of-fact tone she felt both relieved and piqued. *Just all right*? "Should I say thank you?"

"Hm. Well. I've not had much practice giving compliments, I suppose." He held up a piece of pale blue paper. "I take it this is your handwriting?"

With an immediate flutter in the pit of her stomach, Brenna recognized the sheet of stationery on which she'd written her "bill". "I…yes, it is. Did you—"

"I certainly did read it, if that's what you were about to ask. Found it just outside, on the path, and thought it was rubbish."

"It was just a joke," she said faintly.

"I don't find it a bit funny." He held the paper up and began to read aloud. "For services rendered, I charge Michael Larkin the sum of: One walk, with appropriate details given concerning the formation, use of, and methods for gathering turf in the bogs. One hike into the Twelve Bens, lunch to be prepared by said employee. One excursion along the beach, complete with tour and historical lecture on Grace O'Malley's castle. One trip to County Mayo to search for my great-grandmother's old home place—" He looked up, one eyebrow lifted, his mouth barely containing a grin. "You don't come cheap, do you?"

"Look, I said it was a joke. I never intended for you to see that," Brenna said, feeling very much at a disadvantage.

"Doesn't sound like a joke to me. Tell me about this last request."

His tone was so interested, almost kind, that Brenna's defenses went down. "Oh, I told you the other day. Dad has always wanted to come to Ireland, but somehow just never did. I told him I'd try to find the house his grandfather used to tell him about." She had a musing little smile on her face, remembering. "I've seen her picture, my great-great grandmother Maura."

"Yes?" Michael's eyes on her were watchful, his expression speculative, almost as if he were seeing her for the first time.

Brenna nodded. "She was a tiny woman, not even five feet tall, but I gather she was strong-minded enough to make up for her size. The stories my grandfather told about her would make your hair curl."

Michael raked a hand through his hair. "Not any more, please," he said with a grin.

Brenna privately thought that his hair was beautiful, but she continued, "At any rate, I promised Dad I'd try to find the old home place, and maybe talk with any living relatives that might still be in the area."

"Which is?" he asked politely.

"Achill Island in Keen Township."

"Beautiful country," he commented, then suddenly changed the subject. "Are you tired already of your bargain to work for your bed and board here? Is that the reason for this?" He waved the blue paper in the air.

"That's not it at all. I just want to see some of the things in the area, and I never intended for you to see that, please believe me."

"It isn't the sort of business arrangement I expected," he admitted. Brenna knelt to the floor, gathered her things, and started to leave, completely at a loss as to what to say next. He stood also, however, and laid a restraining hand on her arm. "I've offended you."

"No, no, you haven't. It's just that I—" His nearness forced her to take a deep breath. "Look, I only spent an hour on the books. That would be ten or twelve dollars, or..." In her confusion she couldn't figure the amount in pounds.

"Five pounds, or thereabouts," he supplied quietly, looking deep into her eyes.

"Yes, that's more than enough, and I'll be happy to work at them from time to time, as long as Seamus isn't feeling well and I'm here." She was relieved when his hand fell away from her arm. In control once more, she added quietly, "Michael, he has a temperature, and I'm afraid he's coming down with something. Molly is with him, but I ought to check and see if he needs anything. Molly is bringing dinner later." She left then, before he

60

could say anything more that would make it necessary for her to think. Somehow she found that thinking wasn't always easy in Michael Larkin's presence.

Chapter Five

Dinner that evening was a relaxed, pleasant meal; the Irish soda bread lesson which Molly gave Brenna yielded a lovely brown loaf which was devoured to the crumbs. Because Seamus by his own admission had not felt well enough to come downstairs, the meal had been a lap affair with the old man holding court in his bed. As Brenna took his wicker tray she remarked, "Molly's stew was as good or better than any I've ever eaten, didn't you think so, Seamus?" They were the only ones left in the room, as Molly had commandeered Michael to help her take the dishes down.

"Hm. I'm certain it was. Molly's a dab hand at cooking, especially stew. But you gave me too much," he grumbled.

Brenna started to protest that she had actually given him very little, then decided against it. If his appetite was poor, it only meant he wasn't feeling well, and she certainly didn't want to aggravate him. Instead she asked, "How about a fresh cup of tea?"

"Capital idea, Brenna." He looked up at her, all traces of grumpiness absent for once. "It's nice having you here...seems as though you've been here always." He didn't add that he liked having her, but she chose to believe that he did.

She patted his shoulder, concerned at the flushed

look of his face. "I'll get your tea."

Downstairs she interrupted a private conversation between Molly and Michael, because they both stopped speaking when she entered the kitchen. Determined not to show her considerable curiosity, she said, "Oh, I'm glad you're making tea, Molly. I told Seamus I'd bring him a fresh cup."

"I'll take it up, dear. Michael has other plans for you." She smiled brightly as she arranged cups and saucers around the sturdy brown pot with blue stripes that was Seamus's favorite, and airily left the room before Brenna could reply.

"What did she mean?" Brenna asked, watching Michael's face, for he wore a casual wait-and-see expression.

"We're going for a walk." His eyes didn't meet hers; he seemed to be studying some point beyond her shoulder. "I wouldn't want it said that I shirked my responsibilities. After all, a debt is a debt."

"Oh, you're thinking about that list." The evening had been so pleasant, with no talk of politics or personality clashes. Molly seemed to have a good effect on both men, and Brenna hated to see things deteriorate. "Please, Mr. Larkin, let's not drag that up again." The smile on her face was genuine but a decided effort. "I wasn't serious."

"Ah, but I am. It's only now dusk, an excellent hour to see the bogland for your first time. Have you a light wrap? The sky is clear, but Irish weather is notorious for its instant changes." The expression on his face was pleasant, but Brenna sensed rightly that nothing she could say would change his mind. Besides, she did want to go. So she murmured something about being back in a moment, and he inclined his head a bit, saying, for all the world as though they were the greatest of

63

friends, "I'll wait for you outside. Laddie is hovering about, waiting for Molly. Perhaps we'll take him along. I'd like to see how he's using that leg."

He was at the gate, the dog close by his feet, when she came out with her coral cardigan flung loosely around her shoulders. Laddie was obviously keen on taking a walk, and just as obviously had been told to sit and stay, for his body quivered in delighted, suppressed anticipation. "He's ready to go," said Michael.

"And so am I. Thank you for asking me."

As though she hadn't spoken he gazed at the sea, where a small cloud drifted toward them. "As I was saying, Irish weather is extremely changeable. However, I think it altogether true that the rain threatens to fall more than it actually does." He began to walk, and Brenna fell in beside him easily, her stride matching his. "The sky is always changing. Sullen one minute, bright and beautiful the next."

"Didn't I read somewhere that you Irish boast of soft rains?" asked Brenna. "Where I come from we have what are called gully washers...far from soft, I can tell you." She was thinking that for all its unpredictability the weather couldn't hold a candle to Michael Larkin. But she much preferred this mood to his others.

He nodded, his hands thrust deep into the pockets of his tweed jacket, his dark eyes on the horizon. "Yes, and the boast is well founded. And as for remembering something in a book, I seem to remember reading that we Irish and our weather are drawn in tense suspension between bright dreams and tense reality."

Brenna glanced at him in pleased surprise. "That's a beautiful way of putting it."

"Yes, well." He cleared his throat, and as they were approaching a fork in the road he took her arm lightly, indicating they were to bear left. "You'd best be on the

64

lookout here. It's said that the Pookah, the black horse of the Devil, rides the wind to carry off those who venture onto the bogs at night."

"Surely not while Laddie is along to protect us," she answered lightly, noting the sudden lurch in her midriff at the touch of his hand on her elbow. "Tell me about the turf. That is what I smell burning, isn't it?" The soft summer air was delightful, and as they approached a donkey-drawn cart laden with what she supposed were blocks of turf, Michael nodded and called out a greeting to the driver.

"Good evening, Joey. How does it go today? Looks as though you have your quota, and then some."

The man's somber, weather-lined face brightened as he recognized Michael. "Aye, that I do, Michael Larkin. We've gotten a good section this year, a good one indeed."

"Joey, I'd like for you to meet a...a friend of mine from America. This is Brenna Ryan."

The man swept off his cap in a definite, courtly gesture, holding it over his heart for a moment as the smile reached his eyes. Brenna held out her hand, and Joey took it with that same courtliness. She could almost hear his heels click; but he wore a ragtag assortment of clothing which gave no credibility whatever to his princely manner. "I'm very pleased to meet you, Joey."

"Ah, but not as pleased as I am to meet you, Miss Ryan. A friend of our Michael's, eh?"

The knowing look he threw Michael made Brenna say hastily, "Mr. Larkin was just telling me about the turf. What did you mean about getting a good section? Are there bad ones?"

"Yes, to be sure. Walk along with me?" he asked. "I must be gettin' on home or Mikey will be worryin'!" The little donkey responded to a gentle nudge from

Joey, and the threesome walked companionably behind the laden cart. "There's good bogs and bad bogs, and they are given out by the Land Commission. We all of us pay a small annual rent, and a family's luck in the draw is an important factor in our lives."

The dusk was softly gathering, and Brenna felt a sense of quiet contentment and belonging that made her almost sigh with happiness. "Well, what makes a good bog, anyway?"

"Ah, an ideal bog has an even, dry surface, is thick and black with no rocks and such." He turned to Brenna, and she could see the twinkle in his eyes, even in the dimness. "And it's near a good road so's a man doesn't have to break his back entirely and altogether gettin' the sod upon the cart! Sure, and I suppose every man must work some, but there's limits, you know. I'm really a lazy sort."

"How much do you need, for a year, say?" asked Brenna.

"I can tell you that," put in Michael. "The average household uses about twelve to fifteen tons of turf a year, and it takes about a hundred and sixty work hours to cut, dry, and transport that turf—so don't let Joey kid you about his being lazy."

Joey laughed. "Ask my brother Mikey about that, he'll tell you a different thing altogether. Say, we're about to the house. Will you stop for a bit?"

Brenna looked enquiringly at Michael, who said, "Would you like to?"

"Very much," she assured him.

As Joey was unhitching the donkey he called out, "Mikey! Come out, we've visitors."

A man with an equally agreeable smile came to the door, wiping his hands on a towel tied about his middle. "Come in, come in, the kettle's at—"

Laughing, Brenna interrupted. "—at the boil!"

The two brothers, obviously twins, laughed heartily with her as though they understood the joke. Michael stood a little apart, watching Brenna charm his friends and thinking his own thoughts.

Once inside the tiny, sparsely furnished cottage, Brenna looked curiously around her, fascinated by the small curtained alcoves on either side of the fireplace which served as bedrooms, the shelves cluttered with various souvenirs and curios, tea sets and blue willow patterned bowls. A round-faced mantle clock which chimed discreetly on the quarter hour had its own shelf high on the whitewashed wall. By the clock hung a plainly framed picture of the Virgin Mary, dressed in flowing draperies made of that bright blue so favored by Irish girls, and a very Irish-looking, bearded Jesus, his feet bare. Altogether the room had a welcoming air, the dark green linoleum worn but clean. And it all had a timeless look, a look of having been that way for generations.

The four of them sat around the little square kitchen table, laughing a great deal about not very much. The two brothers had never married and had lived in the house of their father and grandfather before them. A turf fire burned brightly in the fireplace, and the only other light was from a small kerosene lamp on the table.

Mikey proudly brought out a crusty loaf of soda bread he'd baked himself, and Brenna agreed that with homemade butter slathered on it, she'd not eaten better, not even Molly's. "I think it's wonderful that you two get along so well without—" She halted, wishing she hadn't spoken, being outnumbered by bachelors as she was.

With what Brenna thought must be a finely honed sense of innate courtesy Joey said, "Sure, and you were about to say without a woman, were you not. Well, Mikey and me would have married, had a pretty lass like yourself come along, but somehow it never happened. We both inherited this small wee house and bit of land—and the problem has been the land was divided into three halves...our half being the worst of the lot!—and the struggle to keep it goin' made us put off marryin'. You must take that fact under advisement, Michael," he finished slyly, with a meaningful look at Brenna.

Mikey pushed another slice of currant-laden bread toward Brenna. "As it is, we get along fairly well without a woman about. The only thing is, it does get a bit cold, of a winter night." A grin twitched his mouth. "Sure, and this is home and all, but these old cottages can get mighty cold and damp...would give a wild duck rheumatism!" They all laughed, and Mikey added simply, "But even if he is me own brother, we get on."

"I think that's marvelous," said Brenna.

"Say, Mikey," said Michael, "tell her the story about brothers being loyal."

A smile lit Mikey's face and with obvious relish he began the tale he'd told many times before. "You see, it's like this. There were two farmers over at the pub at Dunaff in Donegal. One of them said he knew a man who could jump fifteen feet backwards."

Brenna giggled. "Fifteen feet?"

"Exactly," assured Mikey solemnly. "Well, the other farmer said it was quite literally a physical impossibility, that there wasn't a man on earth who could perform such a feat. 'And how could you think that I would believe such a desperate falsehood? If you are telling the truth, just tell me his name, I'd like to know.'" Mikey's face was full of his smile as he said, "The first farmer said quite calmly, 'Why, your own brother Paddy.' At that the second farmer said, 'Why o' course and Paddy could do it. Many's the time I've seen Paddy give a jump backwards not only fifteen feet, but sometimes twenty, or twenty-three feet!' "

Their laughter had not died down when Joey asked if they had heard about the man in Kerry who... And he was off on another tale, obviously enjoying himself enormously.

It was quite dark outside when Michael said, "We really must be going," and rose from his chair by the fire.

Brenna shook each man's hand in turn, genuinely touched at their gracious hospitality. The walk home, with Laddie gratefully frisking after his long, patient wait, was as pleasant as their visit had been. "I can't tell you how much I enjoyed that," she said as they retraced their steps to Crosswinds.

"They say you're really accepted if an Irishman invites you into his kitchen," was Michael's quiet reply. He seemed to have relaxed considerably.

"Then you must have accepted me, because I spend a lot of time in your kitchen," teased Brenna.

"Hm. And you may be right," came the thoughtful answer.

They walked side by side in the dark easily; there was no moon, but the stars kept the night from being black. "Is there a danger that you'll ever run out of turf?"

"I've read somewhere that at the present rate of use there is enough left for five hundred years. But it is a question people are beginning to consider more now than a generation ago."

"Why is that?"

"Oh, before the oil crisis the cutting of the turf wasn't as crucial. But now even the power station at Screeb is utilizing turf, and they're cutting it with machines." He shook his head. "It was intended to provide employment for men who hand cut it, and now where it has been stripped away, the soil is rocky and poor. Ireland is a tiny island with little to offer its people."

"And you love her completely and deeply," said Brenna softly.

"That I do." His words were as quiet as her own. "But when I see how hard a family must work to wrest the turf from the land, as they do their crops and their livestock as well, I wonder that any of us stay. So many emigrate, to live a bit better or to have steady work. There is a joke in Dublin about the German settler in Kerry who has become so thoroughly Irish that his sons have gone off to work in England." He kicked at a stone in the road and then added, "It's to the point that the men far outnumber the women. Just consider Mikey and Joey."

"So the women can take their pick of Ireland's finest—" began Brenna, realizing too late that she'd left herself open for sarcastic retort.

But the visit with Mikey and Joey and the quiet of the evening had evidently relaxed Michael's guard, for he merely said, "Perhaps," then fell silent again as they walked. Almost as an afterthought he said casually, "Some say that marriage is merely an institution designed to help people endure problems that wouldn't exist if they weren't married."

She wasn't surprised to hear him make such a statement; however, she was amazed at his tone. He seemed to be merely repeating an oft-heard adage, not needling her. So she let the observation pass, even though she had her own opinions on the subject.

Brenna's parents had had a very good marriage, and Brenna's yardstick was their happiness, part remembered and part absorbed in the day-to-day living of her childhood. She fervently hoped her father's new marriage was as happy. Ruefully she thought of her beloved parent. No matter how glad she was for her father and Celia, she still felt a sense of being shut out, of longing for someone who would love her as wonderfully and completely as her father did Celia, as he had her mother.

She sighed, affected deeply by her thoughts as well as the wild lonely beauty of the countryside that was so different from any she'd ever seen. Accustomed to the lush growth of her semi-tropical home, this harsh loveliness with its low, bushy vegetation and rock-strewn landscape gave her a strange, lonesome feeling. She shivered a little and pulled her sweater closer.

"What is it?" said Michael, anxiety in his voice now. "I certainly hope whatever has Seamus abed isn't getting to you, too."

The genuine concern he showed was more difficult to deal with than his insults. "I…no, I'm not getting sick. Really, I'm disgustingly healthy, hardly ever catch things. It's just…everything here is so beautiful it makes me want to cry."

"Ah, now, and don't be doing that!"

His dismay was obvious, even though she could not see his face clearly. She laughed. "Don't worry, I won't."

"That's good." He resumed walking, then asked, "Ireland is very different from your own home, I suppose."

"Very. I'm absolutely captivated by it all."

"But I suppose that you much prefer Texas? I've heard that the people in your state have an enormous, peculiar pride about their homeplace."

"That's true enough of most of us, I suppose, but I must be a turncoat. All I can think about is how wonderful it is that the sea is just over there, and even while

71

it makes me feel lonesome, I love the hills and the narrow roads with everyone riding bicycles instead of millions of cars on six-lane freeways—" She halted, a little embarrassed.

"Don't stop. I feel much the same," he prompted gently.

"It's just that there's never any place to be private or solitary at home. I live in a marvelous, very modern apartment complex with security guards and saunas, dishwashers and trash compactors and microwave ovens. All very modern and...and hectic." She gave a great gusty sigh. "I shouldn't be complaining. Houston is one of the most progressive, up-and-coming cities in America. Things are happening there, people are pouring in from all over, and there are fortunes to be made for those who are willing to pay the price."

"And what is that price?"

"Twelve- or fourteen-hour work days or worse, the ability to see what it takes to outwit your competitors no matter what, the conviction that money is the most important thing in the world."

"And money isn't important to you, I suppose." There was a hint of mockery in his tone now.

"I didn't say that. But if it overshadows everything and becomes the single most important thing in your life, I think it's wrong!"

He chuckled and she knew she'd been baited successfully again. "Now, now. Why do you suppose I'm practicing in an out-of-the-way place like Clifden? Sure, and partly it's because Seamus has a good reputation here, and I'm building on that. But I could go to Dublin, or to England even, and do better, at least financially, if I chose. Only I don't. I want to live in a quiet place where people know and trust me. Where there is time for things other than work. We're not as far apart

72

in our approach to life as you think.

"Do you know what a *ceili* is?" he asked abruptly. When she shook her head he said, "It's an evening of traditional music and dance, the old songs and jigs and reels. They used to be called *hoolies*."

"Sounds marvelous—"

"They are. We'll put it on the list."

The list again. Brenna wasn't certain whether that list was a blessing or a curse, but it seemed to be firmly entrenched in Michael Larkin's head. The remainder of the walk home was companionably silent, which suited her. Michael's statements had given her plenty to think about. They were, indeed, closer in their ideas about life in general than she'd supposed; this pleased her inordinately. And it would seem as though he had appointed himself her official guide to the lovely Connemara country. A pleasant prospect, she had to admit.

Chapter Six

By the next afternoon even Seamus admitted wearily that he needed a doctor. The dapper little man who came in response to Michael's summons was, obviously, from the conversation between him and Seamus, a very old friend. But friend or not, Dr. Duffy was adamant in his grave instructions that Seamus behave himself. His diagnosis of influenza was accompanied by strong admonitions of bed rest, fluids, and a careful watch over his diet.

"At your age, Seamus, you must be especially careful," he repeated as he packed his stethoscope and blood pressure gauge back into his bag.

"My age!" snorted Seamus. "You're forgettin', I suppose, that I am the same age as you, Duff?"

"Yes, well. It's not me that has caught the bug, it's you, my friend. Where is Mrs. O'Malley, anyway? A good dose of her barley broth would help about now." He cast a questioning, though kindly, nod toward Brenna, who in the confusion of the examination and diagnosis had not been introduced.

Michael, quietly hovering nearby as though he were the parent and Seamus a sick child, spoke up. "This is Miss Ryan, Duffy. She's helping out while Mrs. O'Malley is with her sister."

"Yes, yes, I'd forgotten she was to be away."

"Aha!" crowed Seamus. "Forgot did you? Now who's getting old? And as for the lassie here, American or no, she's a dab hand."

"Well, I hope she's had some experience at nursing, for you're going to need some close care these next days," Dr. Duffy gravely pronounced.

Michael shook his head. "No, I can't have that. She's here on holiday, in the first place, and Seamus talked her into acting as his slave, cook, and bottlewasher, and as though that weren't enough, she has been at the books—" He stopped, too late.

Seamus glowered fiercely as he said, "So you've been doing my job, have you, lass?" At her brief nod he went on. "Well, let it go, and some of the other things too, as I like having you about, and if I must be coddled, I want you to do it. How about it?" He seemed to hear himself and for a moment his face was that of a small boy as he struggled with his pride. "Please?" he asked, and Brenna knew he was remembering that first day when he'd used that word as a last resort.

Brenna smiled at the naked appeal in his gruff old voice. "Dr. Duffy, I haven't had any nursing experience, but if you'll just tell me what to do, I'm sure I can manage."

"But—" Michael saw he was losing and showed little grace in the process.

"Now, Michael," warned Dr. Duffy, " 'tisn't easy to get someone reliable to come in, you should know that. If Miss Ryan is willing, you'd best let her and be grateful till you can find someone." At Brenna's silent nod he said, "And now, Seamus, are you up to being beat at checkers?"

Michael left the room then, and Brenna followed him down to the kitchen. "Mr. Larkin," she began, "I know you don't feel it's right for me to be here, and I'm sorry about that. But the fact is, I am here, I get along quite well with your father, and he needs someone. Can't you…well, can't you make peace with the situation?"

He busied himself at the sink for a minute, filling the old copper kettle with water, wiping it carefully before setting it on the stove. When he turned to face her, his eyes were serious and intent. "Miss Ryan, I can't deny I thought it was a ridiculous way to go about hiring a domestic, even a temporary one. However—" He turned on the gas flame, adjusted it carefully, and hesitated a moment before he continued. "However, I must admit things go better since you came. It's quite pleasant, actually, and I—" Once again he halted, and Brenna felt sorry for him.

"It's all right, you don't have to explain," she said gently.

"No, you're wrong, I do. My behavior has not been the best, I know that." At her look of quick agreement he gave a rueful grin. "If you'll tend Seamus during this bout, I'll make it worth your while. He seems to have taken quite a fancy to you."

"And I to him," she said. "Mr. Larkin, I came here by accident, but I stayed because I wanted to. And when you act as decent as you are at this moment, I can truthfully say I'm enjoying this 'holiday' more than I have any other."

"But how can you? You're missing all the sights, everything that was advertised on your tour. All you do is cook and clean and work. How can you say you enjoy it?" He was honestly perplexed, as he leaned against the old pine table, arms folded in front of him.

"It's really simple." Brenna sat down at the table and looked up at him, pleased at the earnest look on his face. "I have a very good job with a large oil firm. My salary is a great deal more than what Seamus offered me, even though you probably thought it was too much." He had the grace to flush a little, and she shrugged and went on. "But I don't get the opportunity very often to do what I'm doing here. I get up every morning before six in order to be on the freeway by seven-fifteen, so I can be at my desk by eight-thirty. I rarely go out for lunch; I take it with me or I eat in the company cafeteria, and I work very hard for a very demanding boss. He's an important man, and I can honestly say he couldn't do his job if I didn't do mine. By the way, I'm an administrative assistant, not a secretary, and I'm good at what I do."

"I believe you." A lock of his hair fell forward as he nodded tersely.

"And when I get home, finally, after an hour or an hour and a half on the freeway with people who act like refugees from an insane asylum, I don't feel like cooking, or doing housework, or anything beyond making a sandwich and falling asleep before I finish it. I make good money, but Mr. Larkin—"

"I think it's time you called me Michael, if you're going to bare your soul," he said dryly.

Stung, Brenna said quickly, "I'm sorry."

He ignored her apology but said, more gently, "What were you about to say?"

She felt her lips curve in a little smile at his interest. "I was just going to say that I like to make people comfortable, to bring order out of chaos, whether it's the kitchen or a sickroom or a set of books. I like cooking, and even cleaning, because it makes me, and everybody else, feel better when a room is orderly and smells good. I went to work to prove I could, to prove I could go out and compete in the world and do well. And now that I have, perhaps...." She hesitated, then went doggedly on. "Perhaps I'm ready for something else."

The open look was gone from his face, replaced by one of wary cynicism. "So, we come full circle. What you want now is for some poor man to come along and provide you with a free meal ticket, right?"

"Mr. Larkin, you're impossible! Just a few minutes ago you were worrying about my working too hard, and now you're accusing me of wanting a free meal ticket." She stood so abruptly she almost upset her chair. "You are not only rude, you're downright illogical!"

He stalked to the sink and stared out the window, his hands jammed in his pockets. Finally his deep voice ground out, "Seamus wants you here, so that's the way it'll be, I suppose. But I'll see that you're paid for the extra work you do."

"That's not the point!" Brenna was dangerously close to losing her temper; she didn't do it often and always regretted her words when she did. With an effort she calmed herself. "Look, I don't know what problems you've had to make you think the way you do. But they aren't my problems, and I won't accept responsibility for them. Maybe we're just too different to get along. But I'm here because I told Seamus I'd stay. So if I need to keep out of your way, I can certainly do that. But you'll have to make an effort to stay out of mine, too." He turned and looked straight into her flashing eyes, but Brenna's chin was set defiantly.

For one long, uncomfortable moment, they glared at each other. Finally, Michael seemed to realize the next move was up to him. His eyes still meeting hers, he said slowly, "Miss Ryan...no, I'm going to ask if I may call you Brenna, as Seamus does."

She bit her lip, unwilling to unbend yet, but wanting to be polite. In a low voice she said, "All right."

He nodded, cleared his throat, and said, "You're absolutely correct. I do have some problems that have nothing to do with you, and I do react illogically, and I am rude. I'm sorry. Please, forgive me?" At her little nod he put out his hand. "Friends. And I want your assurance that you will take time off every day, to make sure you don't overtire yourself." She put her hand in his, and he shook it warmly, slowly. "Molly will spell you, I'm certain. And we'll check off some of those things on the list."

"I wish you'd forget that silly thing," she murmured, wondering how long he intended to hold her hand and exactly what had prompted his change of attitude.

"Not a chance. I've a notion it's the best way we may have to show how much we appreciate what you've done." He grinned. "I didn't realize we had a highly paid executive on our modest payroll."

She withdrew her hand from his. "I shouldn't have spouted off like that. I don't know what came over me."

"I do. Except for my ill temper, my illogical boorishness, my rudeness, and my other terrible qualities, I'm really a nice fellow, and you enjoy talking to me."

She laughed outright. "Mr. Larkin, you're—"

"Michael."

The quiet, vibrant sound of his name rang in her ears. "Michael, then," she said softly. "I don't know if—"

Dr. Duffy appeared at the door, and she turned to him as he cleared his throat. She thought his gaze was somewhat speculative as he gave her instructions concerning Seamus. She also knew that, like everyone else, the good Doctor Duffy was curious about the American that Seamus had installed in Mrs. O'Malley's place. She hoped he would chalk up her giddiness to being a "flighty American" instead of the real reason—which was the mish-mash of conflicting feelings Michael

Larkin had created within her. But she was afraid she might as well hang a sign around her neck.

The house was very quiet. After Dr. Duffy left, Michael had been called out, and Seamus, grumbling but obeying her decree that he nap, fell asleep. Brenna, in a very busy three-quarters of an hour, tidied the sick room, washed the dishes, and found herself with a welcome space of free time. She poured a cup of tea that Seamus would have rejected as not near hot enough, and curled up on the loveseat in the parlor. But before she could drink the tea the phone rang, and before she could finish a rather terse conversation on the phone, the doorbell chimed.

"Yes, Mr. Collins, I'll see that Mr. Larkin comes out right away. Sir?" She listened carefully, trying to decipher the thick Irish accent of the caller and to ignore the insistent door chimes. "You think the foal is laid wrong, and the mare is weak from trying to deliver. I see. Well, Mr. Larkin will be able to—what's that? No, Seamus is ill, it'll be Michael." At the small silence on the other end she added lamely, "He's quite capable, as I'm sure you know. I'll give him the message." She hung up, wondering at herself as she hurried to the front hall. How in the wide round world did *she* know if Michael were capable.... Then she smiled; she knew.

She opened the door to a thin, pinch-faced man no taller than herself. He was dressed in a sort of speckled tweed suit that bagged at the knees and showed signs of having been his favorite or perhaps his only one for many years. He was not smiling, but his eyes registered clear surprise at the sight of her.

"Is Larkin t'home?" Even his voice seemed thin and reedy.

"Do you mean Michael or his father?"

80

"Doesn't matter, ah've come to pay on my account."

The question on his sunburnt face was so obvious, she smiled as she stepped aside. "I'm Brenna Ryan, and I'm helping out for a while. Seamus is not well and Michael has gone out, but I was just going over the books and could mark your account if you like."

He stepped inside, but not before he took a long, appraising look at Brenna's dark shining hair and her trim figure in rose colored slacks and white blouse. As he followed her down the hall he remarked under his breath, "Quite a change, quite a change."

As they entered the parlor Brenna turned. "Excuse me, sir?"

"Ah was just wonderin' where Mrs. O'Malley had got to," he said, his eyes meeting hers briefly, then skittering away.

Brenna explained yet again as she opened the book, then realizing he'd not told her who he was, gave him another smile (which had a rather peculiar effect on him) and asked him his name.

"Ah...it's Bailey, George Bailey," he said, a silly, bemused expression on his pinched face.

"And you wanted to pay in full." She thumbed to where she found his name, surprised at the amount, and missed his swift look of consternation. "That will be twenty-seven pounds, fifteen pence." She looked up, still smiling warmly as he drew out his scruffy wallet and extracted several bills, one by one, and placed them on the table. "Thank you for bringing it in, Mr. Bailey. It's wonderful to see a man take his responsibilities seriously. I admire that." Mr. Bailey swallowed visibly, then drew out four more bills and laid them beside the others.

He nodded numbly and turned to go. "Ah hope auld Larkin is better soon." He cast an unbelieving eye at the money she was counting and putting in the cash box. "Shouldn't wonder he's better straight off, after that."

Before Brenna could ask what he meant, Michael came in and the two men greeted each other. When George Bailey had gone she said, "Mr. Bailey came to pay his account up."

"Pay it up? You mean *all* of it?" asked Michael incredulously.

"Why yes, does that surprise you?" she asked, a little puzzled at his reaction.

"Surprise me? It confounds me! Old Bailey hasn't paid up in the thirty-odd years he's been calling Seamus. What did you do, hold a gun to his head?" He looked down into her eyes, his own bright with humor and delight.

"Oh, I just assumed he wanted to pay in full and told him the amount."

"And smiled at him, I'll wager."

"Yes, several times, I think."

"Ah, Brenna," Michael said very softly, "your smile is downright devastating. Poor Bailey never had a chance."

Brenna looked back into his eyes as long as she could, then turned away. "There...there was a call from a man—Mr. Collins, I believe he said—whose mare is having difficulty foaling. I told him you'd come as soon as you could."

"Right. I'll call Molly to stay with Seamus. You get your sweater; it's misting out."

"I beg your pardon?" Brenna said, suddenly dismayed at his closeness.

"You're coming with me." He strode purposefully back to the surgery, and Brenna supposed he was going to get the instruments he might need.

Chapter Seven

Not stopping to reason whether she should be going or whether she wanted to, Brenna soon found herself beside Michael in the battered blue Austin.

"I'm sorry about the mess. Laddie sometimes goes with me on calls since my own dog died. It's been lonely without him, so Molly shares."

"What happened to your dog?"

"Old age." He gave a little sigh. "Lancelot was a Corgi, a wonderful dog."

"Lancelot?"

He glanced over at her, hearing the not quite controlled note of amusement. "He was a true gentleman, and the name fit," he said stiffly.

"Oh, don't be hurt, I think Lancelot is a marvelous name for a dog!" She giggled and was relieved when he laughed too. "Are you going to get another?"

"I certainly am. Have her all picked out. I'll take her home as soon as she's old enough. It won't be long now."

"That's good. Everyone ought to have a dog."

"Do you?"

She shook her head. "I used to when I was growing up. We always lived out from town and had plenty of room for animals. But the owners of my apartment building almost consider it a concession to allow people, much less dogs."

"Don't you miss having a dog?" he asked.

Brenna was touched at the concern in his voice. "I do miss having a dog, very much. And I miss a lot of other things too. City life is hard on a country girl."

"I'll wager you don't miss the mess a dog makes," he said with a wave of his hand, indicating the golden brown hair on the seat and the well-chewed bone on the floorboard.

"Oh, that kind of thing doesn't bother me."

Thoughtfully he said, "That's very interesting." He concentrated on driving for a few moments, then began telling her what an incredible feat she'd accomplished in collecting the whole of George Bailey's debt. "He has the reputation of being the tightest, stingiest man in three counties. I've known Seamus literally to gnash his teeth at the shenanigans Bailey has pulled over the years to get out of paying full price for services. You're a miracle worker. We'll have to give you the hard cases from now on. Might make us rich, you might."

From now on. Brenna heard the words, and a pang shot through her. Michael had spoken as if she were staying forever, and she knew all too well that wasn't possible. She pushed that bit of cold reality aside and said, "How far is it to the Collins place? He sounded very anxious."

Michael nodded, his eyes on the narrow road which was winding into the hilly country beyond Clifden, away from the sea. "Yes, I'm certain he did. He's a conscientious stockman, takes it all very seriously. This mare is his favorite, and a good one, too. I only hope we can save the foal, for I know how much it means to Collins."

"There's a chance, then, that you might not be able to?"

"Ah, there's always the chance, I suppose. With a breech presentation in a cow it's not so critical; you only turn the little creature round. But it's the legs, the lovely long legs of a foal that presents the problem, you see." He glanced at her, no sign whatever of animosity in his manner, his lean face animated only by the thought of the challenge ahead.

Brenna nodded. "I suppose a broken leg is always a frightening danger. The only time I can remember my dad being really mad at me was when he found out I'd taught my horse to walk cattle guards so I wouldn't have to get off and open so many gates."

Michael frowned. "How did you do that?"

"I'm ashamed to say I put a board across the bars and enticed him to walk it with his favorite feed. He didn't seem to mind, once he got the hang of it. I can honestly say I didn't realize, as kids usually don't, how dangerous it was for him. His name was Francis."

This brought a laugh from Michael. "And you dared to giggle at Lancelot?"

"Well, it was my favorite aunt's name, and she was named after my grandfather. The horse really wasn't worthy of the family name, I guess. He was my first, and Dad bought him at an auction for twelve dollars." Her voice was wistful at the memory. "But nag or no, when Dad got through lecturing me I never let old Francis walk the cattle guards again."

"He may not have been the finest horse of the day, but he was smart enough not to break his leg," put in Michael dryly.

"True. Most of my waking hours were spent with that old horse in the rice fields, just the two of us. Then, when I was older my father bought me a really fine little

85

white mare—" She stopped, suddenly aware that she had been talking a great deal and probably was boring the man to tears.

But he showed no signs of boredom. On the contrary, he chuckled again and said, "I'd like to have known you when you were a girl. Riding was something I enjoyed, too. We'll have to find a couple of horses and take a picnic one day."

"That sounds marvelous." Brenna was relieved when they swung off the main road and his attention was diverted to navigating the rutty side road. Michael Larkin, rude and unreasonable, was easier to deal with than Michael Larkin, easy and interested in everything she had to say—or Michael saying her smile was devastating.

The little man who came striding out of the low, long stone structure bore out the impression she'd had of him over the phone. He wore a pair of tweed knickers and a baggy, hand-knit sweater that looked as though the patches on its sleeves had been put there out of necessity, not for sporty decoration. A peaked cap was pulled low over his eyes but failed to hide his anxious look.

"Ah, Larkin, I'm that glad to see you. Lady should have foaled long ago. You know—" He paused for a second as he realized Michael was opening the car door for someone else, but if he was surprised to see a pretty young stranger with the vet he evidently didn't have the time to show it. "You know what hopes we have for this foal, Larkin, its sire being the Emperor."

After introducing Brenna to the anxious Collins, Michael explained as they followed him to the barn. "The Emperor is the favorite stud hereabouts."

"And very dear his services are as well," muttered Collins. "Not to mention Lady is the best I have."

They entered the dim interior of the ancient barn, and Brenna looked around. Old as it was, there were unmistakable signs of a careful man who made the most of what he had. Knowing there was nothing she could do to help, she retreated to the far side and watched Michael prepare to execute the difficult maneuver of turning the foal. He laid out his instruments, washed his hands carefully in the basin Collins provided, and then stripped his shirt off for the work ahead.

For an instant Brenna felt something close to shock at the sight of his lean, well-muscled body. She had been attracted from the first by this obviously better-than-average-looking man, but she had not expected to be so shaken by the smooth strength of his back and long arms. Her eyes did not leave him throughout the whole process. Struggling and panting slightly, he finally managed to turn first one long leg, then the other of the foal. The mare, who had almost given up her own natural efforts to expel the foal, seemed to realize the man's skill had made a change. She gave a huge heave, and the foal was born straightaway, practically into Michael's arms.

"Is he all right?" asked Collins warily, for he had been hovering nearby, silent and watchful.

"Yes, yes, he is!" answered Michael, jubilant that the colt was wriggling in his arms. "He was awfully quiet a bit ago, and I thought he'd struggled too long to be born. But he's going to be a fine colt, Collins, a fine return for your investment."

"Aye, I'm that glad, I am. And Lady?"

"She's fine, too. Probably won't happen that way again." Lady, seeming to sense they were talking about her as a mother, nuzzled the newborn as Michael laid him in the straw beside her.

Brenna felt the sting of tears. The miracle of birth was

a marvelous thing to see, and she was even more moved by the knowledge that without Michael's assistance, both colt and mother might have been lost.

Collins was deeply grateful, and Michael's face, as he washed up and donned his shirt again, reflected his own pleasure at a job well done and appreciated. He declined Collins' offer of a cuppa, saying, "Another time, another time, for I've another stop to make."

Brenna didn't ask what he was referring to, only allowed him to hand her into the car with pleasant courtesy. A man of contradictions he was, puzzling and totally fascinating to her. "That was a wonderful experience, Michael. I can't thank you enough for bringing me," she said as the Austin topped the rise in the road coming away from Collins' place.

"What's that?" he said, glancing over at her. "Oh, you mean the foal. Yes. Well, I can honestly say I never tire of it…the miracle of birth. Almost makes me believe."

Brenna tried to see the expression on his face, but his head was angled away from her. "Believe what, Michael?" she prompted gently.

There was a long silence during which he navigated the rocky ruts skillfully. Just before they reached the turn onto the main road, he stopped the car and looked out broodingly at the still-sweet green of knee-high grass. "Oh," he said finally, "some of the things Molly is so serious about. I don't know exactly how to say it. Maybe God's plan in the world—or if He has one, something like that?"

"Then you do believe in God?" breathed Brenna, almost afraid to say the words.

"Of course I believe in God," he said, looking at her now. His brows, though dark and finely shaped, drew down, giving him an uncanny resemblance to his father. "Whatever gave you the idea I didn't?"

A Scripture verse she'd learned long ago flashed into her mind. *The fruit of the Spirit is love, joy, peace, longsuffering, gentleness…meekness, temperance…*Not many of those qualities did Michael Larkin show. She stared into Michael's deep brown eyes, not at all sure what to say next. When she did speak her voice was low, but fairly steady. "Do you remember earlier today when you were waiting for Dr. Duffy to tell us what was wrong with Seamus?"

"Yes, I do. What are you getting at?"

"Didn't you feel that in a way, your roles were almost reversed, and it seemed as though you were more like the parent and Seamus the child?"

Michael rubbed his neck and leaned his head back against the seat. "I'll have to admit I've had twinges of feelings like that at times, and yes, I did this afternoon. It's not a comfortable thing, either."

"No, it isn't," she agreed. "But relationships change, just as we do, as our needs change." She hesitated, but not for long, before she added, "And our relationship to God changes, too. It can't be static. To be what He wants us to be we have to find out more and more about Him, and the only way we can do that is to know His Son." She stopped, aware of the sudden stiffness in his manner; his hands on the wheel tightened until the knuckles showed white.

Yet he didn't voice his antagonism, although their relationship might have been easier had he brought his thoughts into the open. Instead he merely said, his tone polite but distant, "I'm sure you're right." He started the car and pulled out onto the main road. "I hope Seamus is better."

That was safe ground, and Brenna heartily agreed. In her heart she wondered if she could have done better, if she should have said more, and decided no. "Molly and

89

Seamus have a really special friendship, don't they?"

"Molly is special." A smile quirked his mouth and he added with a sidelong glance, "It's a bit like what we were speaking of before, about the colt being born. Molly almost makes a believer of me. She's not what you call the average religious woman." He halted, and before Brenna could think of a reply, he added a surprising comment. "She also makes me think there's truth in a poll I once read, that concluded that deeply religious women are also very passionate." His face dead serious, he looked over at her. "Seamus has already tagged you as religious. Are you proportionately passionate?"

Flustered, Brenna said, "Why, I'm—" Then she saw the glint of amusement in his eyes. "You're teasing the wrong girl, Michael. My brother and father saw to it pretty much that I know how to take it." She smiled sweetly. "As to whether or not I'm…proportionately passionate, I don't intend to tell you, and there's no other way you're likely to find out, now is there?"

"Hm. Perhaps not." He was chuckling now, obviously taking the fact that she'd bested him at the little game with good humor. "Well, that's a moot point. I'll say this, I've known some notable exceptions to the so-called rule that religiosity equals passion." He was suddenly sober, and Brenna was sorry to feel the easy camaraderie slipping.

In an attempt to salvage the lighthearted mood she asked, "When we were at Collins' you told him we had another stop. What did you have in mind?"

"What would you say if I told you it was a surprise?"

"I'd say I love surprises," she answered lightly. She noted that treacherous little lurch had returned to her midsection and wondered if she ought to insist instead that they return to check on Seamus. But she didn't.

Consciously she tried to relax and take in the lovely, wild countryside they were passing through. But her mind raced with the equally lovely, though somewhat wild, flashes of memory—Michael, stripped of his shirt working with such intensity to turn the foal; Michael's strong hands manipulating Laddie's hip; Michael's teasing, challenging looks just now. How Nola would laugh if she could read her mind at this instant. She tried very hard to banish those thoughts and almost succeeded. Aloud she said, "You know, it seems as though I've been here much longer than I actually have."

"Yes, it does, doesn't it." His voice was low, and he kept his eyes on the road. "I'll have to admit I'm glad Seamus cooked up the plan to have you stop, though at first I was certain it would be a mistake."

Her hands were shaking, but she only said, "It's been wonderful. Usually when you go on a trip or a vacation, it's totally exhausting. I'm sure the tour I started would have ended like that, with me more tired than when I began. And I was plenty tired, I can tell you. My job is…" She trailed off, not wanting to say just how disillusioned she'd come to feel about her job and her entire lifestyle.

"You're not completely happy working in that office, are you?" he asked quietly.

She started to say, *Of course I am; it's challenging, and I've worked hard to get where I am…* but she surprised herself by saying instead, "No, I suppose I'm not. But after spending time in Clifden with you and Seamus I know I'll be ready to tackle it again."

"Will you, now?" murmured Michael. "I wonder."

There were both quiet for a time, and the late afternoon sun was fading as he braked the car to a stop, jumped out, and went round to open her door. His hand on her arm made her shiver slightly, but she smiled up at him and said, "It must be getting chilly," knowing the chill in the air was not what made her shiver.

He reached into the back seat for his jacket and placed it around her shoulders. "It's the breeze from the sea. We'll have to go shopping soon for that fisherman's sweater you wanted."

A little frown creased her brow. "How did you know I wanted one?"

"Don't you remember? You mentioned it that first evening you came to Crosswinds." He gazed into her deep blue eyes for an endless moment, then linked his arm into hers as they began to walk slowly up a rather steep hill.

"Oh, yes, I guess I did." Brenna remembered she'd also said she wanted some lace for her wedding dress, but she certainly wasn't going to bring up that item. She saw they were approaching the ruined shell of a cottage. Lonely, roofless, and facing the sea, it came into view as they topped the hill. Abandoned houses always gave her a sense of desolation, a longing to know why they had been deserted and where the people were who had built them and loved in them. "It's so beautiful here," she breathed. Her words ebbed away as she faced the sea, the water dark now, reflecting the darkening sky. The voice of the sea had been muted before, but now she heard the crashing sound of waves and imagined she felt their power surging through the very earth on which they stood. When she could speak again she said softly, "How I would have loved to live here, to see this every day…to watch the ocean and sky change.…"

"My ancestors did. Come, let me show it to you." They picked their way through the maze that had once been a low rock wall surrounding the cottage. The house obviously had been built long ago of smooth, rounded granite stones.

"How was it constructed? There doesn't seem to be any mortar."

He shook his head. "They didn't use any. Each stone was specially chosen because it fit those around it." He helped her over the threshold, ducking as he did so because the doorway was very low.

When they stood inside, the lowering gray sky was the only roof overhead. She pulled his jacket tighter around her. The faint smell of lime aftershave and of a slightly sharp, though not unpleasant, antiseptic odor made her a bit giddy. The very essence of Michael Larkin...To counteract its effect on her she said a little breathlessly, "You said your ancestors lived here? Is the land still in your family?"

"No, it passed from our ownership long ago." He put his hands deep in his pockets and went to stand near the narrow glassless window. "The Irish have always felt very close to the earth, to their animals. Did you know many houses had a cow byre at one end of the kitchen?" He gestured toward the other side of the cottage, a smile on his face. "Made the cow a member of the family, as it were. I can understand that; I love animals, and a good thing I do. It's people I have a problem with...or women, at any rate." The last words were spoken so softly Brenna wasn't sure what he'd said.

"Did they cook on the open hearth?" she asked. The fireplace was at floor level and the hearth very wide, wider by far than any she'd ever seen, that was true; but somehow she knew they both were speaking only to fill the quiet.

He nodded. "Usually in the old days they did, and with turf, of course. I've heard the old ones speak of keeping the turf always 'smoored' and ready to flare.

Even when whole families emigrated and left the old home places, so strong was the feeling about it that the neighbors vowed to keep the turf fires smoored for them till they returned, and of course most never did. The custom came from the saying, 'Once the fire goes out, the house will soon come tumbling down.' "

"The windows are so small," said Brenna. She was thinking instead of the way the wind ruffled his black hair, making him smooth it again and again with those fingers that were so slender for a man of his size—and so gentle!

He stared upward at the vast sky overhead. "And the roof, before the sea winds took it into the next county piece by piece, was made of Sugan grass from the bogs, or straw, or reeds. Reeds sometimes last forty or fifty years..." He trailed off, his dark eyes holding hers steadily. "I'm speaking of cows and hearths and roofs, but I'm thinking of something else altogether."

As he began to move slowly toward her she heard herself say quite faintly, "What, Michael?" She took a step, and another, without conscious effort, and found herself in his arms. Her head was hidden beneath his jaw, her lips were on his throat. She could feel the steady, quickening pulse there, and the slow caressing of his hands, those gentle hands, as they moved from her back, to her shoulders, to touch her face.

He lifted her head and bent his own, then kissed her closed eyes, her cheeks, her mouth. Finally he said, as breathless as she was herself, "Of this. I've been thinking of this almost constantly since that first time I saw you, so concerned about Rankin's dog"

"That's...that's hard to believe," she murmured. "You never even looked at me. I felt as though you were totally unaware of me."

94

He brushed her temple lightly with his lips. "That's not the way I felt at all."

"You hid your feelings well—"

"I'm not hiding them now." Again he kissed her, and had he not been holding her she would have fallen, her knees were so treacherously weak. He murmured against her hair, "Oh, Brenna, I want—"

A small warning sounded somewhere deep within her, and she pulled away. "No, Michael...no."

He took a deep breath and released her. "I hope you don't think I intended—"

She broke in. "Of course not. I just meant I'm not sure about...things."

"Then allow me to tell you. I know how you were feeling when I kissed you, how you'd feel if I were to kiss you again. You felt the same way I did, and if you deny it I won't believe you."

Brenna stared into his eyes; his hands gripped her arms tightly. It was no use. She couldn't deny his words, and he knew it. She twisted away and stumbled to the door of the cottage, with Michael close behind her. She was so acutely aware of his presence she thought she would burst. Finally she turned to face him. "We'd better get back to check on Seamus, don't you think?"

For one endless moment they stood, then Michael said, "Yes, you're right, I suppose." Politely, carefully, he held her elbow as he helped her to the car across the rough, rock-strewn ground.

Chapter Eight

The atmosphere in the car during the ride home was far different than the ride out to see Collins had been. There was a cool restraint between them, an air of interrupted, unfinished business that neither broke the uneasy silence to clear.

Seamus was asleep when they returned, and when Molly told them that she must leave Michael insisted on walking her home. Brenna stood at the foot of the stairs and watched them go, heads close, with Molly earnestly telling Michael of Seamus's condition; she was indeed a good friend to him.

A good friend. Brenna had seen that for herself and knew it was so. But what had Michael said...*she could have been my mother*. So there had been far more than friendship between them at one time—Brenna was sure of it. Love? Michael had not spoken to her of love. She told herself that what had happened in the ruined cottage surely had been no more than an impulse, one that he'd give in to and she had allowed. She stopped at the head of the stairs as she realized she still had Michael's jacket on. Thoughts of his kisses came to her mind and would not leave, no matter how hard she tried to banish them. *I've been thinking of this since the first time I saw you, he said*...she could not deny the powerful attraction she felt to him. Eyes closed, her mind in confusion but rejecting what her heart was saying with every beat, she laid her cheek on the rough tweed, the scent of Michael filling her senses.

A low throaty chuckle jerked Brenna's head up with a snap. Not six feet away stood an amused Nola with a knowing little smile on her face. "And what would you be doing with Michael's jacket on?"

"I...it was—"

Nola laughed out loud, then put her finger to her lips. "Hush, you'll wake Seamus."

"I'll wake him? You're the one!" whispered Brenna, knowing that Nola was quite capable of making any situation more complicated and confusing.

To her surprise Nola came close and put her arm around her shoulders. "Let's go down for a cuppa, dearie. You look as though you could use one, and a friendly ear, too."

Although Nola would have been the last person Brenna expected to befriend her, she had to admit that she did need a friend. So in the warm cozy kitchen she sat while the Irish girl made a fresh pot of tea, admiring her swiftness and economy of motion. When she finally sat opposite Brenna with a steaming, fragrant cup in hand, she said kindly, "Now let me tell you first that Seamus's fever is no higher. He ate a bite of toast and jam with his tea and fell off asleep while I was reading to him. The influenza will surely go on for a few more days, but Duffy says he'll be fine, and I believe him. Seamus is a tough old bird."

Brenna could hear the affection for Seamus in Nola's voice. "You really care for him, don't you?" she said softly.

"Aye, that I do. My own Dad has been gone for so long, and Seamus is the only—" She broke off, and her tone changed subtly as she said, "But speaking of caring, I'll wager I can reconstruct what happened to you earlier." She reached over and fingered the wool of Michael's jacket.

Too late, Brenna hastily took the garment from her shoulders and folded it carefully before she laid it across a chair. "Don't go making up tales, Nola."

"I don't have to make up anything, ducks. It's written all over your face. Let me see…you were outside, somewhere romantic, walking close, and you mentioned you were cold…he put the jacket ever so gallantly on you, gazed into those big blue eyes, and kissed you silly!"

"Please, Nola, don't," said Brenna, her voice very low.

The other girl stopped in the middle of a merry laugh; her eyes grew wide and serious. "Why, dear heart, you've gone and done it, haven't you? You've actually fallen for Michael!"

"That's not true—"

"But he did kiss you, didn't he?"

Brenna's sigh was deep and long. "Yes, he did. And I can't believe the way I felt…I've always been in control of myself, able to control any situation I've ever been in."

Nola nodded, a knowing expression on her pretty face. "It was different with Michael, eh?"

"Yes, it was," Brenna whispered. "I've never felt that way about anyone before, as though all he had to do was…ask, and I'd say yes, whatever it was. It frightened me."

Nola did not answer immediately but studied Brenna, a peculiar little expression on her face. Then she stood up slowly, came around from her chair, and laid a hand on her shoulder. "Would you believe me if I told you I understand, luv?" Brenna nodded numbly, and Nola

98

went on, almost as though she were alone. "Every time I'm away from my Sean I say, Well, I won't do *that* for him, never! But then he touches me, and kisses me, and I find myself off on some stupid dangerous errand that he has convinced me is essential to the cause."

Brenna looked up, surprised. "I'd have thought from the way you talked the other night at dinner that it was your cause, too."

Nola shrugged and leaned back against the table, hands gripping the edge on either side of her. Her eyes were bright, and her voice was low and electric. "Yes, of course, it's my cause too. But there are times when I'd like to leave the cloak-and-dagger to the others, and feel that Sean wants me safe and protected instead of—"

"Instead of being one of the comrades?" supplied Brenna. The look on Nola's face told Brenna that she'd unwittingly touched a sore point. Gently she said, "It's only natural to want to be protected, especially by the man you love, Nola."

"But I *am* his comrade, his partner!" she said fiercely. "I want to share in the danger, whatever he does, I want to share it!"

It was Brenna's turn to say, "I think I understand."

The fire went from Nola quite suddenly and she slumped, the shine of tears in her brown eyes. "Yes, you just might. But at least Sean admits his love for me. Michael has so many ghosts, so many fears, he'll never be able to tell you—"

Michael's quiet voice from the doorway carried an edge of anger. "Tell her what, Nola?"

Both Nola and Brenna started guiltily, but Nola recovered first. With a toss of her head she said airily, "Why, that you can't afford to pay her salary after all, and that you owe me three months' pay already!" She had discarded her dejection with amazing speed, and with hands on her hips, a mischievous, sassy grin on her mouth, Brenna could hardly believe she was the same girl.

"That's not true and you know it, Nola," said Michael, scowling. "You've been overpaid for whatever bit of work you ever do!"

"Ah, but Michael, dear, what about—" She was off then, recounting some obviously well-known incident between the two of them, and before long Michael said something he shouldn't have about Sean. The effect was like lighting Nola's ever-short fuse.

Her eyes blazed as she snapped, "Michael, you're forever saying things that show you are totally ignorant of the situation."

"And how do you justify such a statement when everything that comes out of your empty head is nothing but what Sean has put there?"

"That's a lie! And if I do believe the man I love, what should that be to you?"

"Not much, I'll say, for all you know is what he has told you."

"Which is all to the good, for my side is altogether in the right!" Nola shook her finger in his face, but Michael didn't bat an eye.

"You're wrong, Nola, there must be answers other than the violence of the I.R.A."

"But you, my fine friend, you have none, do you?" She knew she'd scored by the look on his face.

Stubbornly he persisted. "They can't last; an organization built on the principle that murder and violence are the answer can't last."

"Hah! The British announce weekly that the I.R.A. is dead or badly wounded, but they don't understand that only men die, ideas never die, and the I.R.A. is not an army but an idea. And that, Michael Larkin, is true whether you can admit it or not!"

For a moment Brenna held her breath; she sensed that Michael was angry enough to strike Nola. But, jaws clenched and eyes hardened, he strode from the room, slamming the door violently behind him.

Nola's face was all innocence when she turned to Brenna. "Nasty temper our Michael has, wouldn't you say?"

Quietly Brenna answered, "You did provoke him, Nola. I've watched you do it before. Why do you feel you have to?"

Nola shrugged her shoulders. "I'm not sure. Maybe it's because he's so neutral, so passive—"

"Michael, *passive*? I sure wouldn't say he was passive."

"About the Trouble he is," Nola said firmly. "And that's what matters the most to me. When someone is so blasted calm and reasonable about something so important they need to be poked or goaded into action—at least into saying *something*." She eyed Brenna for a moment. "You don't like me very much, do you?"

With as much honesty as she could muster Brenna said, "I think you're a fascinating girl, Nola. It's just that I don't understand you or your cause and I don't know if I can choose sides—"

"Well, you bloody well better if you intend to stay by me, lass—I'll be provokin' you the same as I do our Marvelous Michael!" With that retort she made as dramatic an exit as Michael had, leaving Brenna emotionally exhausted.

Sleep came slowly for Brenna that night. Even after a long, hot soak in the deep, old-fashioned tub she found that her mind would not let go of the day's images. She tried to think of Nola and the surprising way she had revealed her feelings about Sean. If she were in Nola's place she knew she would feel exactly the same: torn between wanting to be a total part of the world of the man she loved and wanting to be cherished and kept safe from the very real threats of that violent, dangerous world.

And there was no stopping the image of Michael's dark eyes, the wind ruffling his hair beneath the open sky inside the ruined cottage, and his lips on hers. That memory was the last conscious thought in her mind before she slept, and it appeared in her dreams again and again. She felt again his arms tight around her, his lean, hard body so near. Her dreams were full of Michael: a tender, loving Michael, with no hint of cynicism or bitterness in him at all.

Chapter Nine

Brenna checked the breakfast tray: teapot, cup and saucer, whole wheat toast with orange marmalade, and Farina, creamy and lumpless, thank goodness. Sam had always complained loudly if there were lumps, and she had a strong suspicion that Seamus would, too.

When she backed into his room after knocking softly, she was greeted with, "About time! A man could starve to death in this house. What took you so long, anyway?" His shoulders were propped up by several pillows, and his face was glowering—but a much better color this morning.

"I'm glad you're improving, Seamus," Brenna said with a smile as she unfolded the green linen napkin and tucked it under his chin, then placed the tray carefully on his lap.

"Humph. I'm not an invalid…or a child," he said, but she noticed he eyed the tray with anticipation.

Michael came from the adjoining bath then. "If she treats you like a child, it's because you act like one and a naughty one at that, Daddy."

Brenna avoided meeting Michael's eyes; her dreams of the previous night were still too vivid to chance showing her feelings. "Not a child, Seamus. I just think sick people have a little grump time coming, as long as they don't carry it too far, that is. Here, I'll pour your tea."

Deflated by her calm tone, Seamus took a sip of the tea, then sighed. "Mrs. O'Malley will never believe you've learned to make tea so quickly." Suspiciously he eyed the cereal. "Does it have lumps?"

"No lumps," Brenna assured him. "My brother Sam trained me well—"

"Anybody home?" Molly's voice came floating up the stairs, soon followed by Molly herself, looking quite different than she usually did. She wore a pale peach print dress, white gloves, and even a wide-brimmed straw hat. "Seamus, you old rascal, have you got everyone in attendance, as usual?"

Seamus scowled again, but Brenna saw the way his eyes lit up at the sight of Molly. "Dressed to the teeth, aren't you, Molly? It must be Sunday."

Brenna's mouth flew open and she covered it with her hand. "It is, isn't it! I completely forgot!" She looked down at her jeans and plain red cotton shirt; they were far from appropriate to wear to church, even the small, informal fellowship she attended at home in Texas.

Michael shook his head, not trying to hide his amusement. "So much for your religiosity. Now about the other, your score is much better, I'd say."

Brenna caught the malicious little glint in his eyes before she said, "I'd love to go with you, Molly, if you'd give me a minute to change." She found herself backing toward the door in acute embarrassment.

"Well, I came to see if you wanted to go," said Molly, "and I certainly can wait a bit. Staying in the house with these two heathens would rattle anyone." At Michael's protest and Seamus's growl, she continued lightly, "Don't be upset, girl. It's completely natural for

104

you to lose track of time in a strange country, and these two are very strange men as well!" She ruffled Michael's hair affectionately. "Come with us, Michael; you'd like the new pastor. He's about your age and a grand fellow."

As she fled to her own room Brenna thought fleetingly how she envied Molly's easy way with Michael. Would she ever be as comfortable? *Probably not*, she sighed.

Brenna still was expressing delight over the simple but warm service when Molly drove her back to Larkins' in her new red Volkswagen. "It was almost like being in my church at home, except my pastor has a much different accent, that's for sure! I loved it all. Thank you so much for remembering to come and get me. If I'd forgotten altogether and missed going, my week would have had—"

Molly interrupted. "A hole in it, right?"

"Right!" Brenna laughed, then grew serious. "How can people do without it, Molly?...worshiping together with folks like those at your church and mine, and praying, and well, just all the things God has for His children?" She hadn't mentioned Seamus and Michael by name, but Molly knew easily who she was thinking of.

"I don't know, dear. I often wonder, and though I've not been shy about telling them, neither has come to the place where they are open enough to accept Him. It's a sorrow to me."

"Seamus?" asked Brenna gently.

"Aye, but Michael as well. I love him like my own son." She braked the car as they came to Crosswinds' entrance and gave Brenna a long, level look. "I do, you know. I love him as surely as he were my own. But

105

there's something missing in him, something very important to a young woman like you...or me at your age."

Brenna felt her heart grow cold; she knew exactly what Molly was saying. "But Molly, it's not as though he and I were...are likely to—"

Molly shook her head. "It's in your eyes when you look at him, Brenna. Watch yourself, dearest."

"I'll be leaving soon," Brenna said, her voice soft and low. "And Michael certainly hasn't said anything." But the sudden memory of those moments in the cottage stopped her words.

"The Larkin men don't change their minds once they're made up," Molly answered cryptically. "Be careful." She got out of the car and went inside, leaving the younger woman alone for a moment.

Brenna sat staring at the lovely old house, with its protective bower of beech trees and clinging vines. This was the kind of house she'd always dreamed of having—a house that should be filled with children's laughter and happiness. There had been no laughter when Michael's mother was alive; of that fact she was sure. There was some deep unhappiness which none of them, not even Molly with all her forthrightness, wanted to share. Brenna felt as though she was on the edge of a precipice, and if she did not draw back very soon she would fall and never stop falling...

"Brenna?" Michael stood by the gate, a large basket in one hand. As she opened the door he came nearer to help her out of the car and remained standing very close. "Did you enjoy the service?"

"Yes, very much. I...I wish you'd been with us." She leaned against the car, trying to fathom his almost festive mood.

Michael ignored her comment. "I've persuaded Nola

to stay with Seamus and made a lunch myself. Will you be my guest for a picnic this afternoon, Miss Ryan?"

Again Brenna felt as though she were on the edge of a precipice. "It sounds lovely, but, Michael, if I go off with you all the time I won't be earning my money!" She tried to make a small joke, but he was so close her breathlessness made it hard to speak.

"I have the perfect solution," he said, reaching inside the car to place the basket on the back seat and gently guiding her back into the front. "We'll just stop paying you, as Nola has already accused me of."

Brenna laughed in spite of herself. "You're preposterous, you know that?"

As he climbed into the driver's seat he gave a wicked grin. "I know. Irresistible, too, I hope." The little VW engine roared into action and he zipped backward, then around, heading toward the hazy blue Maamturk mountains.

"Why are we taking Molly's car instead of yours?"

"Because Molly agreed that a doggy-smelling wreck like mine wasn't the best vehicle to take a young American female on a picnic, that is if I wanted to impress her with my Irish hospitality. I seem to remember losing some points right at the onset."

"But I don't mind dogs, I like them—"

His voice was deep and slightly rough as he said, "I know, I've noticed." He said nothing more as he drove the snug little car expertly and rather fast.

Brenna had that sinking, falling feeling again; she should have made some excuse, she shouldn't have come; she should have...But when Michael broke into song she laughed and watched him as though she could never get enough of his face.

They say that the lakes of Killarney are fair,
That no stream like the Liffey can ever compare.
If it's water you want you'll find nothing more rare,
Than the stuff they make down by the ocean.
  The Sea, oh the sea is the gradh geal mo croide—

"Wait, wait!" she interrupted, laughing, "what in the world did you say?"

He glanced at her and repeated, "Gradh geal mo croide—great joy of my heart."

Somehow the intimacy of his tone, the almost hidden, smoldering look in his eyes made her ask, "Gaelic, isn't it?" He nodded. "And is the sea the joy of your heart?"

"Yes, I suppose it was, until a short time ago." For a long moment he drove silently, and Brenna held her breath without knowing it. Then he began singing again to finish the chorus in his healthy, if not professional, baritone.

Oh, the sea, the sea is the joy of my heart,
Long may it stay between England and me,
It's a sure guarantee, that some hour we'll be free,
Oh, thank God that we're surrounded by water!

"That was wonderful! The only thing is, you're not a tenor. I thought all Irishmen were tenors," she teased. "Now are you ready to tell me where we're going? Away from the joy of your heart, if my sense of direction is working at all. Seamus seems to think women have none, but the other day we went the opposite way—" She stopped, but it was too late. The scene in the cottage was still so vivid in her mind, and Michael's as well, as she could tell from his next slow, thoughtful words.

"No, you're right, we're not going back to the cottage. As for what happened there—"

"You don't have to explain or apologize," she broke in quickly.

"I wasn't going to apologize, and the explanation is pretty clear. It was something I wanted to do. I'm not one to make excuses for myself, Brenna. When I do something, most often I've made a clear decision, so I must take the consequences like a man." He hesitated, then plowed on. "But that doesn't mean you have to take the consequences, too. You're a guest in our home, for all that drivel about hiring you, a guest who's bent over backwards to be helpful. Someone I like and admire more than any woman I've ever known except Molly…and I took unfair advantage of you."

"But Michael—"

"No, let me finish. We're going to have a good time today, I'll see to it. And I promise not to repeat my performance of the other day." He gave a great sigh, as though grateful to have a difficult task over. "There. Do you feel better now?"

"Yes, of course I do," she assured him, wondering why she felt a curious stab of disappointment more than anything. He was absolutely right, and she should feel relieved. Brightly she asked, "Can you tell me where we are going, or is it a secret?"

"It's a very special lake, though it has no name. Did you know by the way, that the largest lake in Ireland, Lake Corrib, is in Connemara? And smaller lakes beyond counting?"

"No, I didn't. As big as Texas is, it has very few natural lakes."

He frowned as he looked over at her. His eyes showed none of the dangerous, banked fire of a few moments before. "How can that be?"

"Oh, there are plenty of lakes, but they're all man-made."

109

"Well, I can assure you that my lake is pretty much the way God Himself planned it. You'll love it. Seamus and I came often when I was a lad, when my mother was alive."

"Didn't she come with you?"

"No," he said. His voice low and thoughtful. "And though I didn't know it at the time, she was the reason Seamus brought me as often as he did. Things were good between me and him—peaceful. He never went at me, just told me right from wrong and expected the best from me. I tried my best to live up to his expectations." There was a troubled look on his face now.

"I think you have," Brenna answered softly. Though he hadn't said it aloud, she thought she could read between the lines. Memories of his mother were far from pleasant. She wondered if he would ever feel free enough to share them with her, then told herself sternly she wasn't going to be with him long enough. But there was today...she could enjoy today. "Now tell me about this lake, what made it special enough to keep you coming back."

When they had spread the cloth on the ground beside the small, jewel-like lake, she saw he had not exaggerated its charm. The lunch of corned beef, cheese, and watercress he'd packed was so gargantuan, even Michael had to admit he'd brought too much. He lapsed into the heavy brogue she'd expected all the Irish to have. "Sure and begorra, we must be invitin' the little people for lunch!"

She laughed with him, refusing a third sandwich. "You'll be telling me next that you really believe in fairies."

He shook his head. "No, I don't, but I'm reminded of the old woman in Derry who was heard to say, 'I don't believe in the wee folk, but they are there.' " They

110

were seated fairly close, shoulders almost touching. Michael looked into her eyes and smiled. "I hope you've had as nice a time as I have. I haven't laughed so much in all of the past five years as I have since you came to Crosswinds."

"I like to laugh," Brenna said. Suddenly she couldn't meet his eyes any longer and began to examine the rounded pink nails of her left hand.

"Yes." He reached for her hand and clasped it in both his own.

Determinedly, with every scrap of will power she possessed, Brenna said politely, "Michael, hadn't we better pack this away? It's been great, no rain for almost two hours, but we shouldn't push our luck." She was half relieved, half disappointed when he stood, walked over to the car, and rummaged in the front seat. When he came back he had a fishing rod and a wicker creel in his hands, a silly tweed hat like a bowl on his head, and a smile on his face.

Brenna burst out laughing, "*Now* what are you up to?"

"Ever done any flyfishing?"

She laughed again as he flopped on the ground, doffed his hat, and began searching among the flies decorating the old cap. "No, as a matter of fact, I haven't. I suppose the closest I've ever come is bass fishing, and that was a long time ago." She suppressed a giggle. "That just may be the silliest hat I've ever seen."

"Oh, there's a world of difference between using those great heavy lures and these. And as for my hat," he put the tweed on again as though it were the crown of England, "Seamus has one just like it, and gave me this one. It's one of the best birthday presents I ever had. Americans just don't have a proper appreciation for the finer things," he added with mock dignity. Carefully he attached a woolly fly to his line and held out his hand. "Come on, before I change my mind."

"About what?" Brenna asked, gladly accepting his offer.

He pulled her to a standing position and, still holding her hand, smiled down at her. "About teaching a woman to cast. Seamus did warn me against it."

Hand in hand they strolled over to the edge of the little lake; Brenna was certain there had never been a more perfect day nor a more beautiful lake. "I can see how you must have loved coming here. The more I see of your country, the more I love it."

He was gazing at the lake, at the soft velvet dark green of the rushes and the bright golden splashes of the iris. For a long moment the only sound was the scolding noises of a small group of baldheaded coots as a sudden movement in the bushes sent them flying. "Yes, I can see that you do. I think that's—" He broke off suddenly and turned to her. "Here, take this, and remember, lightly, lightly. Wait, I'll show you once."

"Once? More like a few dozen times!"

"No, no. See? It's not hard at all." With effortless grace he whipped the almost weightless line several times, then laid the fly delicately on the water. The spot was exactly where he'd intended for it to go, she was quite sure. "See how easy it is? Your turn."

She took the rod gingerly and tried to imitate him as best as she could, but her efforts were awkward and clumsy. Discouraged, she turned to hand the rod back.

"Here, let me help you." He stepped close behind and put his arms around her, his hands over hers on the rod. With that gentle, easy grace he whipped the line a couple of times, and once again the fly settled perfectly on the water.

Brenna felt the strength of his body and the power of

his hands, and knew she must either move away or turn within his arms.

She was saved from making the decision by his triumphant shout. "Look! You've got one!" In the scramble that followed to land a healthy trout, she hoped perhaps he had not been aware of the longing within her. How she ached for him to take her into his arms again, to break his promise before the day was over.

Ashamed of her weakness, she was grateful for the diversion of measuring and gloating over the beautiful fish. "Maybe Seamus will feel well enough to have this for his lunch tomorrow."

"That's a good idea. Try again?"

She smiled and read the eagerness on his face correctly. "Your turn, teacher."

His grin was carefree and boyish. "Sure you don't mind?"

"Quite sure." She didn't add that she would enjoy watching him, but she did most happily. Before the afternoon had slipped away there were three more trout in the creel.

It was almost four o'clock when they returned to the house. Nola stood inside the door tapping her foot in exasperation.

"Here you two have been lolling in the grass all afternoon while—"

"Nola!" protested Brenna, looking to Michael for support. But all he offered was an infuriating shrug of his shoulders, which plainly said Nola was right, and why not?

"—while I have important things to do!"

"Then go about them, Nola. Thank you for helping out," said Michael. There was a surprising lack of sarcasm in his voice.

Nola noticed the change too, and she lost her bluster.

"That's all right, Michael. You know how I feel about your da."

"How is he?"

"He must be better, for he's meaner by the minute," she answered blithely. "I'll be back in a day or so to check on him. See you, luv," she said with a shrewd glance at Brenna. "Been on a picnic, have you. Some of my fondest memories have been of picnics." Then she waved a careless good-bye and was gone, leaving the entryway suddenly quite still.

For a moment Brenna and Michael stood quietly, until she said, "I didn't thank you for taking me today. It was...wonderful." When he continued to stare out the long oval glass in the door, she asked softly, "Why did you take me, Michael?"

He turned then, a little smile on his lips. "Because I like being with you." Before she could reply he walked quickly outside, leaving her alone.

The rest of the day was relatively quiet, with only one call for Michael. He did not ask Brenna to accompany him, and she was relieved and disappointed at the same time. After getting Seamus settled in his favorite chair downstairs—he'd declared his freedom from the confines of the bedroom—she asked if he minded her inviting Molly over for the evening.

"I'd like to start my sweater and she promised to show me how," Brenna said as she tucked a blanket around him. "There. Are you comfortable?"

He patted her hand clumsily. "Aye, that I am, girl. Don't know what we did before you came. And as for whether or no I'd mind if Molly comes over, why, Molly is like the sunshine. Always welcome."

Brenna, kneeling beside his chair, glanced around her. The homely hodge-podge of slipcovered furniture, the worn but still vivid deep red oriental carpet, the

114

collection of china dogs on the mantel with the small fire burning below were enough to make her sigh deeply. "Seamus, you can't imagine how I'm going to miss this lovely old house...and you too, of course!" She rose and smiled down at him.

"And what about our Michael, will you be missin' him as well?" Seamus asked, not bothering to hide the mischief in his eyes.

"Why, of course." Her own quiet admission had such an unexpected impact that she turned abruptly to hide her tears. "I'll go call Molly."

"You do that, Brenna girl, and ask her if she's made a taste of the ginger crisps lately. Or if she hasn't, I'd be pleased with whatever she can bring."

"Seamus, that's terrible!" Brenna chided him. "I'll make you some cookies—"

"Aha," he interrupted with a sly little smile. "You have settled in, haven't you. Fussing at me like you would your own daddy, making promises of cookies. Yes, I'd say you've settled in."

Brenna fled the implications of his words and soon had Molly's assurance that she'd come, provided it was all right if she brought a visitor. When Brenna told Seamus of this provision he grumbled, "Just as long as it isn't that Biddy Malone."

"Why, don't you like her, Seamus?"

"Humph." He scowled fiercely. "That man-eater has been through three husbands already. The poor creatures died in self-defense!"

"And I'll bet she'd like to make you number four," said Brenna with a barely suppressed smile

"Humph," was all he said. "Wait till you see her. I've seen better looking faces on a potato. Oh, and I hope it isn't Biddy Malone."

To his chagrin Molly did bring Mrs. Malone, although

she introduced herself to Brenna as "Bridget." *Biddy* was a childhood name that all three—Seamus, Molly, and Biddy herself—seemed to think perfectly accept-able to call a middle-aged lady of two hundred coy, flir-tatious pounds. At every opportunity she batted her eyelashes unashamedly at the scowling, amazingly si-lent Seamus, until Brenna finally took pity on him and asked Biddy to tell her about the history of the fisher-men sweaters. It seemed to be only one of the myriad of subjects on which she was a self-proclaimed author-ity. Molly, oblivious to Seamus's aggravation, had qui-etly gone about starting Brenna on her sweater with instructions clear enough for a beginner.

As Brenna painstakingly knit-two, purl-two-ed across what suddenly looked to be a monumental project, she tried to listen to Biddy Malone. The woman actually was a fount of information, for all her idiotic simpering over Seamus. "And now, my dear," she was saying, "Were you aware that these lovely patterns actually originated in our very own Aran Isles? Many, many years ago, each family or clan had its own. And when families intermarried—" Here, she lowered her lashes seductively and glanced at Seamus, who scowled and fiddled with the blanket covering him. "—the patterns were combined until they became extremely intricate. There was even a special sweater called the bridal shirt."

"Really?" said Brenna, almost choking on her laugh-ter, for Seamus was squirming under the intensity of Biddy's designing smile.

"Oh, it was to be worn by a bridegroom on his wed-ding day. Sometimes he knitted it himself, but mostly his sweetheart made it." She reached over, took up

Brenna's small beginning, and examined it critically. "That's good, dear, for a novice. Now *I've* been knitting for many years—"

"A hundred or so," muttered Seamus. Molly tried to suppress a convulsion of laughter.

Either Biddy chose not to hear or she was lost in her own train of thoughts for she chattered on, "I feel I'd really like to tackle something special, like one of those marvelous bridal shirts." (She directed another coy glance at Seamus.) "My dear, the simple patterns Molly has worked out for you will be lovely, but there are so many more to choose from. Why, the *experienced* knitters were inspired by things they saw and used every day—ropes, knots, chains, nets, waves on the ocean, vines, berries, shells, driftwood—"

"Brenna, could you make some tea?" Seamus asked suddenly.

"Of course, Seamus. Mrs. Malone, would you mind helping me?" Brenna thought perhaps her invitation might distract the woman, but it was declined. As Brenna made her way to the kitchen she heard Biddy say, "Now, Seamus, you naughty boy, how have you been managing without Mrs. O'Malley? I was in Maam's Cross and didn't know you were ill, or you *know* I would have come to you, if you'd only sent word..."

Poor Seamus, thought Brenna as she pushed open the kitchen door; but when she saw Michael, his head cradled in his arms at the table, her thought changed to another—*poor Michael*. It took every ounce of resolve she possessed to keep from going to him and stroking his dark hair and those tired, slumped shoulders. "Michael," she said softly, "are you all right? You aren't coming down with influenza, are you?" She filled the kettle and lit the burner, anxiously watching him as he straightened up and rubbed his temples.

"No, I'm not getting sick. Just a little tired, that's all." Yet the expression in his eyes had more than fatigue in it; as he watched her shake out the tea leaves, he spoke slowly. "You should have been with me this afternoon."

There, she heard it again…something in his tone. "Oh, did you deliver another foal?"

"No, pups. Seven, and to the sweetest little terrier you could ever imagine. The couple to whom she belongs have no children, and they were especially anxious since it was her first litter. I wish you could have shared the birth with me. They were so happy."

There was no mistaking now; the yearning in his tone was so plain it twisted her heart. "Michael," she said, swallowing the lump which swelled her throat, "I only have another week here."

He stared moodily at the sugar bowl on the table. "I've been thinking about that." He arose, prowled around the kitchen, and then sat down again; for a moment his face showed his struggle clearly. "You left the tour. Why should you limit yourself to their time schedule? Why not…stay a bit longer?"

Brenna met his eyes. "I can't, Michael."

"Why not?"

"I…I have a job, and—"

"Which you don't really want to go back to," he interrupted. "Is there a man waiting for you?"

The sudden, almost angry question startled her. "Why, no, there isn't."

"Then why not stay on," he said doggedly, and somehow Brenna knew quite suddenly what it had cost him to say the words.

She started to speak but was glad the kettle began to whistle, for she was not at all certain what she wanted to say. When the tea was brewing, the tray set out, and

118

she had nothing left to do, she drew a deep breath. "Michael, there isn't anyone waiting for me, that's true. But I…do you remember when I first came, and I told you that there is a special man for me, that God knows who he is and I have to be open to His leading?"

Michael's dark eyes held hers with an almost painful intensity. "I remember. What does that have to do with your leaving?"

"Well, it seems that the best place for me to be while I wait on God is…is where I've made my life, my own little niche."

"I see." There it was again, that smoldering look in his eyes. He stood suddenly and smiled. "Who's in the front room? I'm almost afraid to ask, but do I hear Biddy Malone?" At her little nod, he grinned. "Poor Seamus. She makes a play for him between each husband."

"Some women never learn," Brenna said lightly as she picked up the tray. He held the door open for her and stood deliberately, she was certain, so that she had to brush his arm as she went through. She wondered if he felt it too…the shiver of intense pleasure that went through her. She knew quite well that he did, and wondered what in the world she would do.

Chapter Ten

Although Seamus looked fit to be tied, the indomitable Biddy Malone arranged to spend the entire next day with him before she left that evening. "I must make up for my terrible neglect of a dear, dear friend," she twittered plainly in the hall as Michael escorted Molly and Biddy to the front door.

"And what kind of son do you call yourself, allowing me to be victimized by that...that—" Seamus thundered as soon as Michael reappeared in the parlor.

"Lovely lady friend?" Michael supplied rather maliciously. "Now, Daddy, you need the companionship of your friends."

"Humph! Molly won't even be here, for she's busy tomorrow. My only company will be that *man-eater*, whom I do not need by any stretch of the imagination. All I need, Michael, is our girl Brenna here. Now *she's* a good companion. Doesn't talk overmuch, and she's tidy, too."

Brenna, who'd been enjoying the conversation as she quietly gathered up the tea cups, hid her smile as she said, "Even if you do make me sound awfully dull, Seamus, I'll protect you."

"Oh, no, you won't. He'll have to fend for himself on this one," said Michael, dropping into his favorite chair opposite his father. "If she's agreeable, Brenna won't be here tomorrow, and neither will I."

"What!" The word was like an explosion. "What do you mean?"

"Yes, Michael, I'd like to know that, too," said Brenna. "What scheme have you got cooking now?"

For answer he slowly withdrew the now much folded and refolded piece of blue stationery. "And I quote: 'For services rendered, I charge Michael Larkin the sum of...One walk with appropriate details given concerning the formation, use of, and methods for gathering turf in the bogs.' Check. 'One hike into the Twelve Bens, lunch to be prepared by said employee.' Check, and *I* prepared the lunch. 'One excursion along the beach.' Next week, perhaps. 'One trip to County Mayo to search for my great-grandmother's old home place...'" He folded the paper and replaced it in his shirt pocket. "Tomorrow will be a perfect opportunity to find out if there are any of your Ryans left. We'll leave early to have plenty of time to ask about."

Brenna frowned, hands on her hips. "Why do you still have that silly list?"

"I'm a man who always pays his debts, and if you think otherwise you do not know me very well."

Seamus looked at his son keenly. "And what would that piece of paper be?"

"Oh," said Michael with a little smile, "a business arrangement between me and Brenna."

"Business arrangement," grumbled Seamus. "If I was your age that's not what *I'd* be makin' with a lass like Brenna."

Brenna, having laden the tray as much as she dared, fled to the kitchen after saying, "A trip to County Mayo sounds like a good idea to me, Michael. Though I'll certainly miss visiting with Biddy, won't you?" Seamus's mighty growl followed her into the hall.

Michael, true to his word, had them on the way to

Achill early the next morning; so early, in fact that they had no time whatever to visit with the incoming Biddy. They met her tripping up the path as they were leaving. Her curls bobbed cheerily as she yoo-hooed good-bye, then marched purposefully toward the house to brighten Seamus's day.

Safely in the car, Brenna allowed herself a small giggle. "Poor man, she'll bully him unmercifully."

"Good for him. He does his own share of bullying, that's for certain."

"Oh, he's a dear. He doesn't bully me."

"You're different," Michael said with a sidelong glance that gave his words more meaning than the light conversation merited.

Brenna smiled, but she made no reply. She was quiet as they left Clifden and traveled north. When Michael had mentioned today's excursion her first inclination had been to refuse, but two thoughts stopped her: she wanted to go, for her own sake as well as for her father's, and she couldn't, no matter how hard she tried, refuse an opportunity to be alone with Michael. Besides, driving through the wild west, as she was beginning to call it, was wonderful. How very different this was from the wild west in her own country!

"I'm surprised that there aren't more trees, when there's so much soft rain all the time," she said as they traveled the lonely stretch between Letterfrack and Leenane.

"Oh, there were more trees, long ago. Man, not nature, is responsible for a great deal of the desolation of Ireland. We've never had the vast timber resources of your country, but had you noticed how the word *derry* shows up in place names round about?"

"Yes, I have, as a matter of fact. What does it mean?"

" 'A stand of oaks,' more or less. But the British used our timber for profit and purposely stripped the land so they could flush out the woodkerns, the last of the bands of forest men."

"The fighting Irish," murmured Brenna. "I have an uncle who, if even half the stories they tell me about him are true, would fight a buzz saw when he was a young man."

"I'd like to meet your family."

His quiet words unsettled her; she could think of no suitable reply so she only said, "Well, there may not be many trees, but you've got a bumper crop of rocks."

"True, true!" said Michael, laughing. "I remember a story—"

'I'm beginning to think everything reminds an Irish-man of a story," teased Brenna.

"So now, and do you want to hear it or no?" he asked in a mock hurt tone.

"Yes, I do, please tell me," she coaxed.

"You talked me into it. Once I met an old man on the road to Roundstone. We leaned against the rock wall on the side of the road and had a nice chat. The Irish love to talk, you know."

"I know," Brenna assured him solemnly.

He shot her a curious look, then continued. "As you've noticed, there was stone everywhere, great hunks of it slicing the fields, tall slabs stepping to the sea, and not a tree to be seen. I said by way of conversa-tion, 'Too bad there's not a market for stone.' And he says, a sly smile on his face, 'Ah, and if it was worth anythin' the British would have long since taken it away and pocketed the profit.' "

Brenna smiled but said slowly, "You're bitter about a great many things, aren't you, Michael?"

"And isn't there a great deal of reason for bitterness? What's to keep a man from getting bitter, when there's so much unfairness, so much inequity in the world?" he demanded.

The answer echoed in Brenna's head—*the love of God*—but wisdom prevented her from blurting it out just then. She knew at that point the angry man beside her would have only scorned her answer. So, aloud she said, "It's really very good of you to take the time to indulge a whim of mine."

"It's not a whim to want to find your ancestors. Those things are important."

"Yes, that's so. But your practice is, too, and I'm afraid you've been spending too much time with me."

"My choice," he said firmly. "And as for my practice, if there's an emergency they can call one of the other vets in the area. I'm not the only one, you know."

"Just the best?" She was gratified when she saw the tension in his face relax.

"Possibly." A smile quirked his mouth. "Well, probably!" They laughed together, and for the remainder of the trip Brenna carefully steered the conversation into lighter channels. When they drove over the causeway that led to Achill, the largest of the islands around Ireland, Brenna breathed a sigh of pure delight. "I know it's not the same as when my great-grandparents lived here, but how beautiful it is." The green slopes of the land seemed to stretch down, down to the ocean, more gently than at other places she'd seen; somehow there was none of the harshness of the land they'd traveled through—only a lovely pastoral setting that was very soothing.

"Indeed it is. Now we must go on to Keel township, am I right?"

"So far as I know." The road from Cashel to Keel was for the most part a lonely one, and she remarked, "What in the world do the people who live here do for a living?"

"Well, some fish, though a great deal of their catch goes to the tables of the rich in Britain and France," he

124

said. "There's not much farming, most of the land is too boggy and hilly. The truth is, because the scenery is beautiful, the fishing is good, and there are excellent beaches, tourism keeps the island alive. And a great many artists have settled here for obvious reasons."

"Hmmm. That's interesting," Brenna said absently.

He reached over and touched her shoulder. "You weren't listening, were you?"

"Of course I was—" She stopped. "Oh, Michael, I'm nervous. What if we do find someone? What will I say to them? Even if they are family, they'll be strangers."

"Don't worry, they'll love you. Who wouldn't?"

And suddenly Brenna forgot any anxiety about meeting her father's relatives, as her thoughts repeated again and again Michael's last two words. Sternly she scolded herself; it was ridiculous to find hidden meanings in every innocent statement Michael made.

As a result of Michael's careful, methodical questioning in several homes, they arrived just after noon at a whitewashed cottage that clung to the rocky side of the island facing the bay. Brenna's heart was pounding as Michael stood back to let her knock at the dark-green painted door. The woman who answered was tall, her gray hair drawn back into a loose bun. She wore a black dress with a crocheted shawl—bright stripes of gold, aqua, rose pink, pale pink, and dark green—crisscrossed over her bosom and tucked into a narrow belt. On her feet were a pair of high-top, black and white basketball shoes. It was the shoes that stayed Brenna's tongue.

"Yes?" said the old woman, her voice soft with age. "And what may I do for ye?"

Still Brenna could not speak. Gently Michael stepped forward and placed a supporting arm around her shoulders. "Are you Meggie Ryan?" At the woman's nod he continued with utmost courtesy, "May I present

125

Brenna Ryan? Her father is John Ryan, who is your husband's nephew."

The faded old blue eyes misted. "Are ye now, *truly*?"

"Yes, yes I am," said Brenna, her throat tight with the tears that threatened her, too. "I've come to visit, because my father always wanted to—"

"Come in, come in! How fine it is that you've come."

They followed her into the dim little cottage. There were only a couple of windows, begrimed by the sea air past cleaning, but Meggie Ryan turned up the lamps and bustled about, insisting they take the best chairs. Swiftly she cleared several piles of crocheted handiwork from each. "I make my livin' that way, child. See, this is to be worn together. If you like it, I'll give it to you!" She thrust it into Brenna's hands, and Michael shook his head when Brenna started to protest. Quickly she realized what he had known at once, that the old woman would be hurt deeply if she were to refuse.

As Brenna inspected the wonderfully intricate pattern of the ivory two-piece dress, Meggie put the kettle on the stove and filled a plate with shortbread. Then she halted. "What am I thinkin' of? It's time for lunch, as Americans see it! Have you had lunch?"

Brenna admitted, "No, we haven't. But we wouldn't want you to bother."

Her newfound relative would have none of it. "Sure, and it'll just be cabbage and bacon, but the bacon is that good." Her eyes twinkled as she added, "The pig was a personal friend of mine. I fair hated to see him go to slaughter. But it was that or no bacon—" She shrugged her shoulders philosophically.

Over the humble but hearty lunch, Meggie Ryan answered all Brenna's questions and some she hadn't asked. How her grandfather's older brother had become a priest and gone off to "blackest Africa," as Meggie put it; how his youngest son Tomas, her own husband, and two sons were tragically drowned all together in a storm almost twenty years ago; how they'd wondered about Brenna's grandfather who'd emigrated to America, for no one knew much about what he'd done or where exactly he'd settled.

"He settled in Texas, Meggie, and had two daughters and a son, who is my father. And I have a brother named Sam, who looks just like Michael here." She smiled at Michael's surprised expression.

"You never told me I looked like your brother."

Meggie looked from Brenna to Michael, and back to Brenna. Shrewdly she said, "It's often that way, girl. When we choose a man it's in part because of a resemblance to someone dear."

"But I haven't..." Brenna trailed off in embarrassment, aware of the intent expression in Michael's eyes. Suddenly she caught sight of an accordion, sitting atop a high, blue painted chest. "Oh, do you play the accordion, Meggie?" she asked to change the subject.

The old woman shook her head. "Lord knows I used to, and very well, I might say, but not so much any more."

"That's too bad," said Brenna. "I'd love to hear some real Irish music."

Meggie frowned, then brightened. "I've an idea. I'll go over to my neighbor's and use her telephone—haven't one of my own, you see—and we'll gather up a bit of music!"

And shortly thereafter a young man with a serious, almost doleful expression and a violin case knocked at the door, followed by two men with no instruments in evidence until they drew out slim silver whistles, and finally a carload of exuberant couples, among them one wonderful accordion player. When they found that the black-haired lassie from America was a Ryan and was wanting a "bit of music," they had a better-than-average excuse to put on their music.

Soon the little cottage was filled with music and clapping, and Michael Larkin's voice was beaten by none. Meggie, clearly delighted with the whole impromptu affair, added to the batch of shortbread an impressive array of goodies and a river of tea. When the last of the merrymakers straggled away, calling out good-byes until they echoed against the sea, the day was gone and a good part of the evening.

"Ah, won't you be changin' your minds and stay the night? It's been that grand havin' you, Brenna, and your young man as well. Oh, can you ever sing, Michael Larkin, like an angel," Meggie said warmly.

Brenna started to deny again that Michael was her young man, but when she glanced up into his eyes she saw the truth. "It's because of Michael that we came, Meggie. He's been wonderful. I may have missed my tour, but he's seen to it that I haven't missed anything important, like coming to see you."

"Yes, indeed, and I can see how wonderful he is," Meggie answered with a smile. "A vet'nary, did you say you were? Ah, that's impressive, a professional man. Well, if you must go, you must. But you'll come again."

It was more of a command than a request, and Brenna was delighted. "I can't tell you how much I'd like that."

Leaving the old woman was hard. After the hours of song and laughter her cottage was all the more still and lonely. But she waved them off gaily, after insisting again that Brenna accept the lovely Irish rose crocheted dress. As they drove away Brenna held the dress up in the dim light of the car and admired the fine stitchery.

"Do you have any idea how much that is worth?" Michael asked. When Brenna shook her head he answered, "About two hundred fifty American dollars, I'd say. Not that she herself would get that much for it, but the boutiques are hot for things like that, quality hand-made things." Dryly he added, "American tourists have lots of money, you know."

"All I know is that it's priceless to me," she said softly. "She's such a dear lady. Oh, Michael, how can I ever repay you for bringing me?"

His voice was strangely subdued. "I can think of a couple of ways, neither of which would involve money."

"Michael..." She felt that treacherous shortness of breath; there were times, like now, for instance, when she thought perhaps he could hear the beating of her heart.

"Relax, Brenna, I promised I wouldn't take advantage of you, and I won't. Why don't you try to sleep? We've a long drive ahead of us."

"But what about you?"

"With all that is on my mind, sleep is definitely out of the question. Here, use my jacket for a pillow."

She curled up on the seat, her head resting on his folded jacket, and drifted off into a light sleep. The next thing she knew was the touch of Michael's arm resting lightly on her shoulder.

He smiled down at her. "I hope you don't mind. I was a bit tired and needed to rest my arm."

"No," she murmured, "I don't mind." *No, I don't mind*, she thought sleepily, *I love it*. His warmth was deeply comforting and gave her a sense of security and of belonging that she was too tired to dispute. For now the one place in the world she wanted most to be was exactly where she was, close and warm at Michael Larkin's side.

Chapter Eleven

As Brenna left the establishment of John O'Donovan, Victualer, with her carefully chosen lamb chops, she gave a little sigh of contentment. Shopping in Clifden was far different from the rush of picking up a few items at the overcrowded supermarket on her way home from work. She'd spent the last half hour pleasantly chatting with O'Donovan and Mrs. Duffy, the doctor's wife, with no feelings of guilt whatsoever. Brenna had one more stop in her morning rounds of Clifden before returning to Crosswinds to set out the lunch she'd already prepared. Dr. Duffy had given her a prescription for Seamus with instructions to find "the chemist's," but he'd neglected to mention that the shop bore the name *Moran's Medical Hall*.

When she entered the small, slightly dim building sandwiched between a travel agent and a solicitor's office, Brenna was greeted by a smiling, snub-nosed young man with gray eyes.

"Good mornin', Miss, and may I help you?"

It was impossible to keep from returning that warm smile, even if she'd wanted to. "Yes, you certainly can. I'm—"

"You're Miss Ryan, and you've come for the medicine for old Larkin, I'll wager," he said, both palms flat on the fine old oak counter as he leaned toward her.

Brenna laughed and read the tag pinned on his spot-less white coat. "Yes, J. Flood, Dispensing Chemist, I am Brenna Ryan, and I have a prescription here from Dr. Duffy." She handed the paper to him.

"Have it in a jiff. How is the vetinary?"

"Much better. His fever is gone, but he's still weak. However," she grinned at the sudden memory, "his appetite is enormously improved. He ordered a dinner that would amaze you."

J. Flood, Dispensing Chemist, busied himself for a few moments as he poured a liquid from a large container to a small one, then carefully hand lettered Seamus's name and a few instructions on a wide blue label. "There. That should do it." When he slid the package over the counter his warm gray eyes met hers. "I'm only his friend, not family or anything, but I can tell you I'm that grateful for your care of the old fellow. We—all of us hereabouts in Clifden—love him for all that he's rascally. There aren't many whom he hasn't helped with one trouble or another."

"I can imagine," murmured Brenna.

He nodded, a faraway look in his eyes. "I remember the time when he delivered my dog Sally of a whopping big dog pup that would have killed them both had he not been there. He's a grand old man, he is."

"Yes, he is. He and I have gotten along very well."

J. Flood eyed her keenly. "Hmmm. And have you, now? He likes people to think he's tough and prides himself on being difficult. We all know better, but strangers usually think him crusty." His mouth quirked as a mischievous look came over his face. "And how have you gotten on with Clifden's most elusive bachelor?"

Brenna felt her own face grow warm. "Why...fine, just fine."

With an appreciative, though not insolent inspection

of her figure, he said, "Is that a fact. Hmm. Well, at any rate, I thank you for being kind to Larkin, and watching out for him. We've all been impressed with how an American stranger can drop so neatly among us and be so at home."

Suddenly ill-at-ease, Brenna stammered something about paying for the medicine she was tucking away in her purse, but the smiling chemist shook his head and said he'd already put it on Larkin's account. So she thanked him and said good-bye, assuring him she'd be back. But as she walked slowly up Sky Road, her mind was in turmoil. So most of the village thought she'd made herself at home here...

Home. Home was a modern condo at 2031 Forest Hill Drive just off Lawndale, nine busy miles on the Gulf Freeway from downtown Houston...wasn't it? Not the wonderful, green-shuttered, two-story house at Crosswinds. She was dismayed to realize how she was hurrying the last few steps, how much she looked forward to entering the sunny foyer. In the wonderful, homey kitchen she sternly told herself, as she put away the groceries, that the room belonged to Mrs. O'Malley and Nola, not to her. Quietly she stood in the center of the room, taking in the wide window that overlooked the little kitchen garden and the wonderful tangle beyond, the black cooking range with which she was now on quite good terms, the scrubbed old table at which she'd spent such pleasant times with Seamus and Molly and Michael—With a rush of feeling she realized how very much these people had come to mean to her. The thought of never seeing them again caused an almost tangible pain in her chest, and though she fought admitting it, never seeing Michael again seemed more than she could bear.

"Brenna?" The sound of his voice in the hall broke

into her consciousness. "Are you in the kitchen?"

She forced herself to answer brightly. "Where else would you look for the hired help?"

He stopped in the doorway, his eyes full of something she dared not name as he caught sight of her. "You must be mistaken, you're far too bonny a lass to be the hired help."

Brenna swallowed with difficulty. "Michael, I—"

But he came over to her and took her arm. "Go with me. I've a call from Bailey and if you're along he'll probably pay on the spot." His hand was warm, and it moved from her elbow to her shoulder almost caressingly.

"You just want me along so you can collect..." She heard the breathiness in her voice, struggled against it.

"Oh, no. I want you along because when you're near me it doesn't matter whether it rains or the sun shines." He leaned even closer, so close she felt engulfed in the smoldering depths of his eyes.

"I really don't know if I should."

He laughed and said easily, "Don't worry. You're safe with me." With one last mocking little grin he added, "At least I think you are."

Outside he bundled her into his car, which was surprisingly clean; there was no dog hair and the floor on her side was covered now by a square of mossy green carpet. He noted her questioning look as he manhandled the car into gear and down the road. "Yes, I cleaned up a bit. Are you impressed?" She smiled, not speaking, and he gave a nod of satisfaction, then broke into a rousing little song that was totally incomprehensible to her because it was all in Gaelic.

"That was wonderful!" she clapped her hands when he'd finished. "I only wish I knew what it meant."

"It's a love song," he said, not looking at her.

133

"Oh, I see," she replied faintly. "Do many...is Gaelic widely spoken here in this part of Ireland? And what about the rest of the country?" *A love song, he said.* She longed to ask him what the words meant but dared not. Better to steer the conversation to other things ...better not to think at all of the sudden, turbulent flood of emotion within her.

"Sadly enough, not too many Irishmen are familiar with it. Since the second half of the nineteenth century there has been a calamitous decline of the national language, at least as it's spoken by the people. Oh, there are societies who work toward preserving it, but it has all but died out everywhere but here in the west."

"Why is that?" asked Brenna, grateful for the matter-of-fact tone in his voice now.

"Ah, life has changed in all ways, so why not our language? The old ways are abandoned by the young in the name of progress."

"That's always the case, isn't it?" asked Brenna, thinking of her own urban existence; how different it was from her quiet childhood in the country.

"Yes, but a people must hold onto and preserve *some* of the old ways, the customs, or they lose their very identity!" he said passionately. "Emigration has caused a sixty-six percent decline in the population of Connemara alone since 1900, especially those who farm the land."

"It sounds serious," said Brenna softly, feeling his pain.

"Yes, it is." He gave a great sigh as he turned from the main road onto a poor, rocky one. "When the land loses its peasantry, the beat of its heart is never the same again."

He shrugged, and a smile lightened his face. "Forgive me. Like Ireland herself, I become a little passionate at times."

"There's nothing to forgive. Men who care deeply about things...and people...are rare and precious."

The glance he gave her was keen, but she met it squarely. Then he said lightly, "Ready for Bailey? I want you to give it your best. How about practicing on me?"

"I don't understand."

"Sure, and I think you do." He reached for her hand on the seat and clasped it warmly. "Smile." His eyes dared her. And when the smile that was lurking spread from her lips to her eyes he smiled back. "Look at us, would you, a couple of ninnies. Anyone watching would say we were in—" He broke off, but the mischievous glint in his eyes spoke the rest.

"Michael, you're impossible!"

"And you rather like *impossible*, don't you?" He cut the engine as they pulled up in front of a sturdy, squat-looking stone farmhouse. Then he bent swiftly and kissed her mouth before she knew what he intended. Just as swiftly he got out of the car and went 'round to hand her out, as though nothing at all had happened.

Nothing? Brenna was intensely aware of the longing she felt, the wish that they were somewhere else, somewhere quiet and private...like the cottage by the sea. But they were at Bailey's, and he was walking toward them, his expression changing comically as he recognized her.

"Why, hullo, I...Miss, uh..."

"Ryan," she supplied mercifully. "We met at Crosswinds."

He gave a huge sigh and a pained look crossed his face at the memory. "Aye, I do remember, I do."

Brenna's smile made him sigh again, and she felt

135

rather than heard the chuckle Michael gave. "I've come along with Mr. Larkin to—"

"To help," Michael said smoothly. "Now, Bailey, where is this cow?"

"Out at t' barn," Bailey said. "But I'm that certain it's no big job. Won't take but a twinkle, and you'll be done with it." Obviously he was downgrading the job in anticipation that the fee would be in keeping with the smallness of the task.

The rocky path over which Bailey led them made for difficult walking, and Brenna felt Michael's hand at her elbow several times. Knowing she must somehow subdue the unruly feeling his nearness aroused, she murmured, "I can manage, Michael."

He stopped for an instant, his dark brows lowered like Seamus, the look in his eyes unreadable. "But why should you, when it's so much nicer to let me help you, and I like doing it so much?"

"Because I want—"

"You don't know what you want, but I do. And it's the same as I want." Before she could open her mouth to reply he put his arm around her shoulders and held her tightly as they walked on to catch up with Bailey. There was nothing she could do but match his long stride.

When Bailey looked back his eyes opened wide at the sight of their closeness, his mouth in a silent O. "Hmmmmm. Interestin'."

"What's that, Bailey?" asked Michael calmly.

"Uh, interestin' case, you'll find this an interestin' case," said Bailey hastily, still eyeing the arm that held Brenna tightly.

"What seems to be the trouble?"

"Ah, something in the old cow's teat, something that disallows the milk from coming through. Her production has fallen off somethin' terrible. Was always good, too," he finished in a mournful tone.

"Doesn't sound like too big a job," said Michael, his jacket off already and his sleeves half rolled up.

"Sure, but she's—" Bailey halted suddenly, and with a quick glance at Brenna he said, "Seamus allus does a capital job. First time for you here, am I right?"

"Yes, that's right. You always insisted on Seamus," said Michael without rancor. "I don't blame you," he added as he saw the look on Bailey's face.

"Me and Seamus, we go way back," defended Bailey.

"Old friends?" asked Brenna with a smile.

Her friendliness had the same effect on the pinched little man as before. "Uh, well, you might say that."

Under his breath Michael muttered, "Old enemies, more like." Aloud he said, "In here, Bailey?"

A vigorous nod, and Bailey led the way to where a gentle-looking cow stood in her stall, placidly chewing her cud. The next few moments brought Brenna to a hopeless state of giggles, Bailey to an unholy smirking satisfaction, and poor Michael to a state of hopping about the stall, muttering oaths that would have made Seamus blush. At his first touch the cow had, in rapid succession, swiped him in the face with a mucky tail, stomped his left foot soundly, and viciously kicked his right shin. She then returned to chewing her cud as if she had never moved a muscle.

As Bailey, trying to look sorry, hurriedly rigged the cow's foot to a rope which attached to a suspiciously convenient ring on the byre wall, he said with a sly smile, "I should have warned you, she's a mite touchy about that teat—" As Michael straightened his clothes and dusted half the contents of the stall floor from his trousers, Bailey gave Brenna a sidelong look of almost sinful satisfaction.

"Yes," was all Michael allowed himself to say as he set to work. "Yes. You certainly should have told me."

With the cow immobilized the job was done in a short time, and as they returned to Michael's car Bailey presented them with another surprise. He gave Brenna one more glance, straightened manfully, and said, "Now, young Larkin, what is it that I owe you? I've a policy, that debts should be taken care of straightaway."

"A good policy, that," said Michael sourly, and named a fair price, considering what had transpired in the barn.

Bailey counted the money out to Brenna, with a comment about how since she was the bookkeeper she'd best take the payment. He pressed her hand for only a little longer than he should, and she smiled at him anyway. He still had the silly grin on his face as they drove away.

Brenna kept her laughter under control for a least a mile. When it erupted Michael grinned ruefully and pulled the car over to the side of the road. "I *was* trying to impress you with my expertise."

"Oh, Michael," she gasped, "you *did* impress me!" Her laughter rang out again, healthy and untainted with self-consciousness. "I'm afraid Bailey got the best of you, though, even if he did pay for the privilege! When you were hopping around, I thought I'd split!"

He gave a deep sigh, then began to laugh with her. Finally he said, "I love to hear you...to watch you laugh."

At his tone she grew quiet and still. "You told me that before. Sometimes I feel I ought to be more ladylike, and not so—"

"No, no, don't ever change," he interrupted quickly. "So many women are the very opposite. They stifle the good, natural things within themselves, and for some reason I'll never understand, cultivate the strangest so-

138

called virtues, usually in the name of religion." He was very serious now, as he gazed out at the lonely countryside. The sun's slanting rays gave a lovely illumination to the wild moorland; in the late afternoon the vast, almost treeless landscape gave forth a feeling of desolation.

Brenna shivered at the intensity in his voice but did not comment. Somehow she knew that he had a need to speak of something, and his next words proved her intuition right.

"When I was very young I sensed something was different about my parents. They didn't argue, nor speak crossly, but neither did they laugh together. The silence, that was the worst part, the silence of them." He stared at nothing for a long moment, then said slowly, "That silence didn't extend to me, however. Each of them in their own way was determined that they would mold me properly. Properly..."

The bitterness in his tone prompted Brenna to interrupt softly, "Michael, don't feel you have to say these things to me."

"Ah, that's exactly how I do feel." He faced her. "I've never spoken of this to anyone—not even to Molly. But I want you to know." A deep, ragged breath tore at him as he continued. "She was at me from the time she woke me in the morning 'til she told me it was bedtime. Do this, don't do that, and never just once...countless, endless times. I never did anything quite right, never. But I could have lived through that, children do. When I finally realized what she'd done to Seamus I decided that a woman, and marriage, were two things I wanted no part of. She systematically deprived him of everything over the years. There was never quite enough food on the table, never quite enough quilts on my bed, or his...." His eyes were brooding as he said, "I've no

139

idea when she stopped sharing his bed, but it must have been very soon after I was conceived. And she was a very religious woman."

Suddenly Brenna understood many things that had been a puzzle to her before. "Michael, I'm so sorry."

He shrugged his shoulders. "The worst part was, there was never, never any love, except what Seamus felt for me, and tried so hard to show me."

"But why was she like that?" Brenna whispered.

He rubbed a weary hand over his eyes. "I don't know. Perhaps because she knew Seamus never really loved her as he did Molly, that she was second choice; perhaps other things in her life that I'll never know. Seamus did marry her on the rebound, you know."

"No, I didn't, though Molly said some things that made me wonder."

"Even then Molly's relationship to God was such that when Seamus refused to allow her to squeeze him into her religious mold, as he put it, she broke off the engagement. They were both sorry, but Seamus immediately began courting my mother to spite Molly, and she accepted his proposal for reasons of her own. The decision very nearly ruined us all." He shook his head, his fine dark brows drawn in a frown. "I may be wrong, but even now I believe if my mother had given of herself freely, if she'd been able to show the love she must have felt, at least in the beginning, Seamus would have put his feelings for Molly aside."

"But she couldn't, could she?" said Brenna. "It's all so sad."

"That it is. She died young, a pinched, dried-up woman whom we…Seamus and I, had to work hard to mourn."

"And you felt guilty about that, too, didn't you." Brenna's statement was quiet—so quiet she wasn't certain he'd heard. As he bowed his head, one hand over his eyes, she felt a pang of sympathy so sharp her own hand went involuntarily to his shoulder, to the vulnerable-looking nape of his neck. He shivered at her touch. "Michael, don't. Don't torture yourself with old guilts—"

His next words were so low that Brenna moved nearer in order to hear him. "I said I'd never allow myself to be put in a position like that—to allow myself to be made less of a man and hurt as deeply as Seamus was, or to bring a son into the world to suffer the same fate."

"Oh, Michael, all women are not like that, we're not!"

He looked up at her then, and caught the hand that had moved to his face. "No," he said slowly, "you're not like that. I've never known a woman like you, never let myself know any woman. You're kind, even when I act beastly, but you don't let me hurt you, even when I try. You're generous, you're bright, you're fun, and you laugh like a man!" His own laughter was low and delighted as he held her face in his hands and looked into her eyes.

Faintly she said, "I'm not sure...is that a compliment?"

"Oh, you can be sure of it! Brenna, lovely Brenna, I cannot keep my promise any longer."

She felt absolutely powerless, not against the dark-eyed man whose lips touched her face so gently, then moved inexorably to her mouth, but against the flood-tide of longing within herself. Never in her life had she wanted anything more than the kisses and embrace of this man. For several endless, blissful moments she knew only that she wanted nothing but for this to go on forever.

He held her tightly, his lips against the smoothness of her tear-damp cheek as he said, "I'd ask you to forgive me for breaking my promise, but I never will be sorry." For another gentle moment he was silent, then he asked softly, "Are you...sorry, I mean?"

She drew away, not meeting his eyes, knowing if she said no he would take her in his arms again and she would be powerless against him. But she also knew she could not be dishonest enough to say yes. So she only gazed out the window opposite him.

When he could bear the silence no longer he said, "We'd best be going. I've another stop." He paused, then added, "It will only be a short one. I hope you don't mind."

"No, no. Of course not." Michael started the car, and to her utter amazement, in a few moments the two of them carried on a perfectly inane conversation about something—she hadn't the slightest memory of what, later—during the ride to his next appointment. She had a painful sense of having lost something very precious.

Michael braked the car at a lovely little cottage that Brenna thought must be the epitome of all such dwellings. With the pleasure plain in her voice she cried, "Oh, it's wonderful! There's even an arch over the gate with roses—"

"Yes," said Michael dryly, "the proverbial rose-covered cottage itself."

"Would you rather I wait outside for you?"

"No, I doubt if Mellie would allow that. She loves company."

"Who's Mellie?"

Her question was answered as Michael inclined his head to a tiny, yellow-haired girl who was running toward them from the rear of the cottage. Michael was opening the door for Brenna when the child, who couldn't have been more than five years old, hurtled herself into his legs, hugging them tightly.

He grinned. "What can I say? At least she thinks I'm wonderful." The sight of his hand caressing the bright hair of the little girl and the foolish look on his face that men sometimes get when they show a weakness well hidden touched Brenna deeply.

Mellie looked up at him adoringly. "Have you come for your pup? She's all ready for you. Come on," she said, tugging at his hand. With another winsome smile she looked at Brenna. "You may come, too. Who are you? A friend of Mr. Larkin's?"

"I…" Brenna met Michael's eyes briefly; the sudden flame of feeling she saw there seared her heart. "Yes, Mellie, I'm a friend of Mr. Larkin's."

"Then come in! Mother's gone to the shops, but my father's here working. Come on!" She took Brenna's hand, too, and nearly dragged them down the flagstone path.

Inside, the little cottage was a pleasant shambles. In the midst of what looked to be a full afternoon's unbridled playtime for Mellie sat an apparently oblivious man in front of a typewriter, crushed papers around his desk like snowballs.

"Mr. Larkin," he said, "it's good to see you again. Excuse the house being so untidy, but Lynne's at the butcher's and I'm babysitting."

"That's quite all right. Wes Connoly, this is Brenna Ryan."

Brenna returned the man's smile and shook the hand he offered, preoccupied with the idea that Michael no longer explained her presence with him. Though he was yielding to Mellie's insistence that he continue on to the kitchen, Michael managed to ask, "And how is the book, Wes?"

"Ah, it's coming. But if I hadn't done a book before I'd say writing one is an impossible job. Mellie, don't be so—"

"But Dad, he *came* to see Jennifer, to get his pup! Didn't you come to get your pup?" At Michael's nod she said, "See, Dad, I told you. He said next time he came the babies would be big enough to take home. I remembered." Her blue eyes were alight with excitement as she ran ahead to the box and picked up a small, wiggly, dark brown puppy. "And here's yours, the best one, 'cause she looks like Jennifer." Carefully she placed the puppy into Michael's hands, then looked up at Brenna. "Are you a very, very good friend of Mr. Larkin's?"

"That she is, Mellie," Michael said softly, "a special friend."

"Then the puppy must be yours, too," she said solemnly. And with that she took the warm little creature from Michael's hands and placed it in Brenna's.

"But Mellie, I won't be—"

The look of hurt that came over the child's face was all too apparent. "But I only give them to special, special people..."

Helplessly Brenna looked at Michael, whose steady gaze said pretty plainly that she was on her own. Finally she said softly, "Thank you very much, Mellie. I'll make absolutely sure she gets the best of care."

Michael knelt beside the child, and from a word here and there Brenna knew he was assuring her of the same thing, the total excellence of the care the little scrap of a puppy was going to receive. It wasn't hard to see that Mellie had Michael Larkin wrapped around her tiny finger.

When he rose Brenna said as much. "I believe you're a softie for little girls."

"Hm. And for a certain big one, too, if the whole

144

truth be told," he said with that glint in his eyes again.

Brenna found she could no longer stand the intensity of his gaze; she was very glad when Mellie said, "May I hold her just one more time?" She gave the puppy to the little girl and watched as she whispered some secret good-bye in its bit of an ear. Then Mellie slowly handed it back to Brenna, saying, "You look like you've got lots of love. Puppies need lots of love, you know."

The sound Michael made could have been a chuckle...or something else. "Well, we must be going, Mellie. Thank you very much for the puppy, and tell your mother we were here. I doubt if your father will even remember."

As they made their way across the cluttered front room Mellie's father looked up, as though it was the first time he had seen them that afternoon. Michael merely waved and gave Mellie a final hug.

In the car he waited until they were a mile or so down the road before he said, "Well, now you'll have to stay. You can't go off and leave your new responsibility, can you?" The puppy was in Brenna's lap, curled between her hands. He had spoken in jest, but a note of something in his voice made Brenna aware that leaving Ireland was fast becoming something she didn't want to do. Yet to stay seemed even more impossible. The entire situation was impossible—especially the fact that she could no longer deny that she was deeply in love with Michael Larkin.

That night as she relived the moving interlude in the car she earnestly asked God for an answer. And as so often was the case, she drifted into sleep with no clear answer from Him, but with the now familiar assurance that He would make the way plain for her...in His own time.

Chapter Twelve

"Molly, I know I should have called...if you're busy I can come back later..."

The older woman took one look at Brenna's troubled face in the doorway and drew her inside. "Nonsense. A friend is never too busy. Come into the kitchen and I'll make a fresh pot of tea."

Brenna followed her through the cozy, cluttered front room, then sank gratefully into the highbacked, wooden chair Molly indicated with a wave of her hand. "Seamus went with Michael today on a call, the first time since he's been sick," she said. "I told him it was a little soon, and he told me to stop dithering." A smile lit her face briefly at the thought of the old man's scowl.

As Molly prepared tea and set out a plate of fragrant triangles which Brenna now knew were scones, she said, "I'm that glad he's better, lass. You've done a wonderful job of nursing him, I'd say."

"I couldn't have done it without you, Molly."

"Nonsense." She sat in the chair opposite Brenna, looked her squarely in the eyes, and said, "It's Michael, isn't it?" A lone tear rolled from each corner of Brenna's blue eyes as she nodded slowly. "You've fallen in love."

At the quiet, matter-of-fact words Brenna suddenly could bear her struggle no longer; she put an unsteady hand over her eyes as the tears began to flow in earnest

"Oh, Molly, you warned me, but I couldn't…it just happened."

"I know, lass, I know."

Something in her voice made Brenna realize the extent of Molly's empathy. "You loved Seamus, too, didn't you?"

"I love him still, and will until I die." The statement was stark and lonely; its finality made Brenna shiver.

"But you refused him." For a long moment Brenna was silent, then she said slowly, "And he would marry you in a moment even now, wouldn't he?"

Molly stirred her tea, which had been stirred already. "Aye, that he would. But I cannot, even as I could not thirty years ago."

"Oh, Molly, here I am faced with the same problem…" She bit her lip. "At least almost the same problem."

Molly chuckled. "I take it he's not actually asked you to wed." At Brenna's rueful shake of her head Molly chuckled again, her eyes bright. "But he will, lass, he will. I've seen the way he looks at you."

"And what am I going to say?" The question was soft, beseeching.

Molly shook her head. "Oh, no, Brenna, it's not me that must be deciding. You have your own life, and you're a great grown girl who must be about making your own decisions. Wouldn't your dad say the same if he were here, or your mum?"

"My mom died before I became a great grown girl, Molly." She wiped a tear from her face. "She was a lot like you."

The sound that came from deep within Molly was no chuckle this time but laughter, pure and simple. For a moment Brenna was startled, until Molly caught her breath and said, "Ah, Brenna, that's a fine, subtle bit of blackmail you're tryin' on me, but it will not work."

Shamefacedly Brenna murmured, "I'm sorry, Molly, really I am."

"It's all right, girl. I understand. You want someone to tell you what to do, and that's perfectly natural. But I can only tell you that for me, being alone the whole of my life was preferable to living with a man who did not share my love of the Lord, and who resisted every effort I made to share it with him." She drew a deep, slow breath. "I do not regret my decision, although so often I've been lonely."

"Then you think I should—"

Molly held up a restraining hand as she interrupted. "No, no, I cannot say what you should do. When the times comes you must have searched your own heart and be ready with the answer that God will give to you. Of that I can be sure, He will lead you; He will give you that answer."

"You're right, I know you are. It's just that it's so hard, and I get impatient." Absently she toyed with the delicate, flaky pastry until there was a pile of crumbs on the china plate.

"Ah, so you don't like my scones," teased Molly.

Realizing what she'd done, Brenna said contritely, "I'm sorry. They're delicious, I'm sure. I'm just not very hungry."

Molly shook her head. "Being in love is not an easy road under the best of circumstances."

"And these circumstances are certainly not the best, are they?"

"I'll not try to lie to you, lass, you know they're not." When Brenna rose to leave she added, "You'll come and let me know what comes about, will you not?"

"Of course I will," Brenna assured her warmly, and went to put her arms around the woman who had so quickly become a real friend. "And with no ulterior motive whatever I want to tell you that you *are* like my mother!"

When she quietly let herself in at the kitchen door at Crosswinds, Brenna found herself faced squarely with her situation sooner than she'd anticipated. Michael appeared in the hall, and his words confirmed her sudden suspicion that he'd been waiting for her.

"I've been listening for you to come in."

"Molly and I…we've been talking," she said, hoping he wouldn't ask if the conversation had been about him.

"I thought as much." He didn't move toward her, but Brenna felt his presence so keenly she went to the sink, with the ridiculous hope that there were dishes to be done there. The porcelain was clean and bare. "How did your call go? Did it tire Seamus too much? Perhaps I'd better to up and check on him—"

"In a moment. I've something I want to ask of you."

Brenna felt a sudden stab of panic. She shook her head almost unconsciously. "Michael, not today."

He rubbed his chin with the knuckle of his forefinger, as though he were trying to read her mind. "No, not today. But I've a trip planned for tomorrow. And before you say no, you should know it's Seamus who insists I take you."

"Seamus?"

Michael nodded. "Yes, he feels you must see the Arans, and I agree."

Brenna made one last attempt to avoid a situation she knew would be difficult and lifted her chin. "Well, I'm not at all sure I can spare a whole day, Michael."

"You can and will," he said with quiet determination. "I want to take you."

She frowned at his near bullying attitude. "Did it ever occur to you that I might not choose to go?"

"But you do want to, don't you?" he asked softly, and though the arrogant assurance on his handsome face infuriated her, Brenna had to admit, "Yes, I do. But—"

With a satisfied nod he said quickly, "Good. I'll make arrangements. It will be a memorable trip, I promise you."

Brenna sighed as he strode from the room; she knew all too well what she'd let herself in for. After she found Seamus sleeping in his maroon plush chair, she slipped out for a long walk. There was a great deal she had to think about, a great many things she had to bring to Him in prayer.

When the next day dawned clear and bright Brenna dressed carefully, knowing it was going to be a difficult but enormously important day in her life. She chose a pretty mauve shirt and slacks. A paisley scarf that echoed the tones in darker shades of wine and rose added color at her throat now, but could go on her head if the weather changed. Low walking shoes of burgundy leather and a light jacket of the same burgundy completed her outfit. She applied her favorite rose blusher and clear pink lipstick carefully, and when she stood before the mirror to appraise the results of all her careful preparations, she was still uncertain. What had Nola said? *Michael thinks American women wear too much makeup....*

But the Michael who was waiting at the bottom of the stairs for her had a look on his face that made her think perhaps she'd done all right. "Ready to go?" He took her hand and held it for a long moment.

"Yes, but Michael, we have to talk."

"Later. We'll talk later, I promise. Go say good-bye to

Seamus. I want him to see how lovely you look."

She knew he was watching as she walked into the parlor, because Seamus's whistle of admiration drew a low chuckle from him.

"We'll be late returning, Seamus," she tried to make her voice sound perfectly normal, despite the storm of emotion within her. "Are you sure you'll be all right?"

"Of course," he grumped. "What do y'think I am, an invalid? Sure and I must look after this snippy pup anyway." He tried hard to look put upon, but Brenna noticed the gentle touch of his big hand on the tiny puppy's head. "You watch that son of mine, lass, he's not to be trusted, even if he is my own flesh and blood. Or maybe 'cause he *is*!" He roared with laughter, and Brenna bent to place a swift kiss on his cheek. "You smell wondrously good, girl."

"Thank you, Seamus. It's some Irish scent that Nola left. She'll probably skin me alive if she finds out I used it. You won't tell her, will you?"

"Me? Certainly not! My lips are sealed. Wouldn't want that pretty skin harmed, that's sure."

Brenna noticed the impatience on Michael's face. "Michael seems ready."

"That he is, girl. As I said, watch him close!"

"Oh, I didn't mean—" Knowing she was caught no matter what she said, she allowed Michael to take her arm and steer her toward the front door. Seamus was still laughing as they went out, and Brenna had the sinking feeling that already she'd lost control of the situation.

The drive from Clifden to Galway town took a little over an hour; the time was surprisingly quiet. Brenna could not keep herself from glancing occasionally at Michael, and invariably he caught her at it. The smile on his face was somewhat enigmatic, and she puzzled over it. Finally, as they drove through Oughterard and headed south, she decided he was enjoying something more than simple pleasure in what was probably quite a familiar drive to him.

"A penny for your thoughts," she said, then amended her statement. "Or should I say tuppence?"

"They're worth far more than that," he answered lightly, "but since they're about you, I'll be glad to tell you…later. I thought we'd do a bit of shopping in Galway, then lunch at the Ardilaun House Hotel."

"When do we go on to the Islands? After lunch?"

He nodded. "I hope you don't get seasick. The steamer that goes from Galway Bay to Inishmore is fairly large, but to get to Inishmaan or Inisheer, which I prefer, you have to be ferried over by curragh."

"Oh, you mean those small boats the fishermen use?" She laughed. "Do you really think I'm up to that? From what I've read you have to be fearless to fly over the waves in them."

"That's almost what they do, too. They ride very high, with almost no draft, and literally glide over the tops of the waves, quite unaffected by the currents."

"I'm the one who'll be affected by those currents," said Brenna with a wry smile.

"Perhaps not. I'll be there close."

"Yes, that's true, isn't it, you will." Brenna was silent for the few remaining miles into Galway; it seemed that every phrase, almost every word they spoke had hidden meanings—with all too obvious implications.

When they drove into the lovely old town Brenna felt she would enjoy every minute of the day's sightseeing with a man who loved his country so well. And enjoy it she did. From the Collegiate Church of St. Nicholas of Myra, where Michael said Columbus himself was reputed to have prayed before he sailed for the west in the

Santa Maria, to the old fishing village of Claddaugh, Brenna was enchanted. She and Michael laughed at themselves, for this was her first time to see the sights and he swore it seemed like his first, because of her enthusiasm. Michael kept urging her to find something she liked, but she resisted actually buying anything.

It was at a tiny jewelry shop that something caught her fancy. "Oh, Michael, look at those rings!" The observant salesgirl, whose dusting of attractive freckles and soft, wavy red hair had probably been an enormous help in landing her the job, took the velvet-lined tray from the display case and stood by as Brenna surveyed the selection. Almost immediately she picked up one of yellow gold, with a design of two hands clasped, holding a heart surmounted by a crown.

As she slipped it onto her finger Michael said, "That's a traditional Claddaugh ring. Long ago they were exchanged at marriages by the folk in the fishing village of Claddaugh. You've picked a pretty one."

Brenna held her hand out to admire the craftsmanship. "Oh, yes. I'll take it," she said to the quiet, waiting girl, who obviously knew her wares would sell themselves.

But before Brenna could even open her purse, Michael had placed the money in the salesgirl's hand. He shook his head firmly at the protest on Brenna's face. "No, you must let me. Part of the tradition is that one never buys a Claddaugh ring for one's self. Isn't that right, Miss?"

Gravely the red-haired girl agreed. "Right you are, sir."

"Well..." Brenna hesitated, then smiled. "Thank you, Michael. I'll cherish it."

He took his change and said, "Now, where would you like to go?"

She thought for a moment, then asked, "Do you know of a bookstore nearby?"

"There's Kenny's, sir," the polite voice of the salesgirl put in.

"Good idea. How'd you like to browse while I run an errand?"

Brenna started to say she'd go with him but changed her mind. "I'd like that. Browsing in a bookstore is one thing I hope they let me do in heaven."

Michael rolled his eyes but said nothing as they left the pleasant little shop. The bookstore was a family affair, with Mother Kenny at the cash register and the Kenny sons waiting and willing to help find whatever Irish items anyone might want. After assuring one of the good-looking fellows that she merely wanted to look, Brenna spent almost an hour of blissful browsing among stacks that she thought surely must be among the best in all of Ireland.

By the time Michael returned she'd found a slim, leather-bound volume of Yeats to replace the one Seamus had given to Molly, and a newer one like it for herself. She'd made certain to pay for them before Michael came; from time to time she touched the gold ring on her hand and thought of him. His dark eyes were amused when he asked if she'd enjoyed her browsing; Brenna's enthusiasm for Kenny's Bookstall knew no bounds.

"I'd love to come back. Once is just not near enough to see everything!"

"Perhaps we can, soon."

Quite suddenly Brenna remembered with a pang all the other wonderful places and people she'd thought of wanting to come back and see again. The lake, Meggie

Ryan, little Mellie…Crosswinds itself.

The dining room at the Ardilaun House Hotel was certainly to Brenna's liking. A pleasant Irish country house atmosphere emanated from its oak-beamed ceiling and chintz tablecloths. She asked Michael to choose from the menu and found the salmon he ordered excellent. They lingered over coffee, which, Brenna realized, was the first she'd had since leaving Texas.

Michael glanced at his watch and rose. "We'd better go. The boat leaves at one-thirty and it's almost one o'clock now. Ready for the great voyage?" He came to pull out her chair, and as she stood she looked up over her shoulder at him.

"Yes, I suppose so." She gave a barely contained sigh; how could she be ready when she didn't know what the next few hours would bring? A little prayer left her heart as she felt his hand at her back lightly, guiding her through the tables of the almost full dining room.

When they were safely aboard the ferry *Naomh Eanna*, their purchases stowed in a string bag, Michael stood close by her side at the rail. Once again Brenna had the distinct impression he was enjoying a familiar experience all the more because of her delight in the beautiful blue water, which mirrored a mostly blue sky. A few clouds were gathering across the western horizon now, which bespoke a possible end to the sparkling day later, but for now the scene was sweetly perfect.

After the boat docked at Inishmore, the largest of the islands, it continued on to Inishmaan, where to Brenna's delight they were lowered into a curragh to be ferried ashore. Amazed that she felt no fear or seasickness, she examined the light craft made of tarred canvas, skillfully rowed by a silent, almost dour Irishman who wore a tweed cap pulled low over his eyes. His intricately knit

155

sweater would have pleased even Biddy Malone, and on his feet were the leather shoes without backs which she'd read about: they bore the unlikely name of *pampooties*.

Michael murmured in her ear that his outfit was for the benefit of tourists like her; his smirk was infuriating when he also told her that most of the real fishermen had abandoned the traditional pampooties long ago in favor of tennis shoes with rubber soles.

"Spoilsport," she murmured back. He shrugged his shoulders and raised his eyebrows.

The ride was exciting but short, and when she and Michael and the other passengers stepped ashore Brenna had such a feeling of times and eons past that she was silent. Michael, carrying the bag, seemed to sense her awe and did not break the silence as they began to walk inland to the highest point of the island.

She had thought the land around Clifden had an unruly rockiness, but Clifden was nothing compared to this barren terrain. As they walked farther and farther it was apparent that Inishmaan, for all its starkness, and despite the sound of the sea around them, held a stillness that she'd never experienced before.

When she finally spoke, her voice was hushed and still. "It's strangely wild and full of peace at the same time."

Michael nodded. "Those who are born here, and leave this place to make their fortunes, or for whatever reason, say that until they return there is no real peace again for them."

As they topped a high, rocky cliff she stood awed at the sight before them. "I can believe that. It…it makes me want to write an epic poem, compose a symphony…oh, I can't say what!"

He smiled. "You're not alone. Men have come here

156

just because of all this," he gestured with an outflung arm, "and the people here, who are truly different, have written great books and plays. I've more a sense of seeing life stripped of all but the essentials, and knowing how important it is for us all, whether or no we are Islanders, to try and do the same in our own lives. Here they must manufacture even the little bits of soil in which they raise their meager crops."

He was standing just behind her, his hands on her shoulders as he spoke. Far below them a man piled hay to dry on the house-sized boulders beside his cottage. The white-washed walls and thatched roof stood timeless and beautiful in their simplicity. Quite suddenly she forgot Michael's comment on the soil, and no longer could she concentrate on the deliberate, methodical movements of the man so far below. She was aware only of the slow, insistent pressure of his fingers as they caressed her shoulders and moved up to rest beneath her hair.

"You have such lovely hair," he murmured. "I bought something while you were at Kenny's..."

Though she heard the whisper of tissue being unfolded she did not turn around; she was rooted to the ancient stone beneath her feet. Only when she felt something brush her hair, and cascade to her shoulders, could she move to face him. Almost of its own volition her hand went to touch the soft, wondrously wrought stuff that he'd draped carefully on her head. The veil was like gossamer fairy wings, woven by skilled Irish hands she was sure. Her eyes filled as she saw the lovely roses and intricate patterns.

"Oh, Michael!"

"It's your wedding veil," he said softly. "Ah, you'll make a lovely, lovely bride, indeed you will." His lips brushed her tear-wet lids and moved to her trembling mouth. When he stopped kissing her he whispered against her cheek, "Ah, lass, I love you, I love you."

Breathless, feeling suspended in time, Brenna heard her own answer, the words small and soft. "And I love you, Michael...but—"

He appeared not to hear that last word as he smiled down at her. "I know you do! That's why I couldn't let you buy that trinket for yourself." His thumb caressed the Claddaugh ring tenderly. "The legend says they must only be given and received in love. When we marry, though, you must choose a proper ring."

"Michael, I can't." The words this time were woefully flat and final.

He was suddenly very still, and quite as though the weather sensed his change of mood and matched it, the clouds began to sweep closer. His face lost its look of soft love and became hard. "Exactly what are you saying?"

Brenna pulled away and was dismayed as she saw the fragile lace veil slip to the ground. She bent swiftly to pick it up, then shook it carefully, folded it, and handed it to him. His eyes blazed with the question, which seemed to hover even yet in the thickening air between them. "I can't marry you, Michael." There, she'd said it, although it had cost her infinitely.

"But you just said you loved me. Was it a lie, a small social lie?" he asked harshly, sarcastically. "Perhaps you do things differently in your progressive country!" His tone made her draw back even further as he almost savagely jammed the lace into the inner pocket of his jacket.

"No, it's not like that at all! I did mean what I said, I *do* love you! But—"

"But not enough to marry me?" Cold, hard words they were, words that chilled Brenna as much as the sharp wind that had begun to blow.

"Please try to understand, there are other things I have to consider," she begged.

"Such as?"

"Such as…as much as I've come to care for you, I also care…even more about God and His will for my life," she finished with difficulty, for his expression was almost frightening. "You're just not…not the right man for me."

"I see. It's come to that, has it. Like Molly, like my mother. I was wrong, I thought you were different. I hoped you were different. But a religious woman is always the same, it seems. Well, your God may make your decisions, but He won't warm your bed, or—" Suddenly he seized her roughly and his lips on hers were bruising, hurting. She struggled, but when he let go of her it was because he was through with her, not because of her struggle. The cold drops of rain had been falling randomly, but now as a dark cloud moved directly over the island it began to rain in earnest. Michael's hair was plastered to his head and he said, his voice quite devoid of expression now, "You can find your way back to where the curragh brought us, I take it?"

She nodded numbly, glad the rain disguised the tears on her face.

"Good. I'll be there." He wheeled and left her where she stood.

For a moment she considered calling him back, even running after him. But she didn't. Slowly, she made her way over to a wide rock and sank down beside it before she gave in to the racking sobs. "Oh, Lord, why? I don't understand…I don't!" The rain was relentless, driving and cold; how long she sat huddled against the ageless stone she could not have said. But something within prompted her to rise shakily and make her way back the way she and Michael had come. Together they'd come, and alone they both returned.

When she saw him standing close to the water's edge, his back to her, staring out at the sea, no words came. Silently she waited until they gave the signal to climb into the small curragh, and silently they rode to Inishmore and on to Galway Bay. There was nothing more to be said. As she shivered inwardly, determined to keep from showing how miserably cold she was to the very core, she realized that whatever had begun between her and Michael was now as cold as she felt. Cold and over, with no hope of rekindling the lovely flame. She'd certainly seen to that.

Chapter Thirteen

By the time they reached Crosswinds the numbing cold had crept into Brenna's very bones. She tried to act as though Michael's casual, offhand attitude was not the most chilling factor of all. At the gate to the house he merely reached across her, opened the car door, and said, "Tell Seamus I've some errands to run and may be quite late getting in."

She stood shivering in the gloom of early evening long after the winking red lights of his car disappeared. She did not deliver the message, because Seamus was not in the house. No one was home, and there was no fire in the parlor. Brenna made her way up to her own room, and after peeling the damp clothing from her body, climbed wearily into bed. Though the sheets were soft cotton flannel she drew no comfort; she felt like a block of ice from her heart to her toes as her unwilling mind kept going over the ill-fated day.

It had begun so well. The beautiful drive, the wandering about Galway, the ring—She twisted the metal on her finger, remembering how Michael had so gravely told her she mustn't buy it for herself, and his explanation later of how they must only be given in love. In love...

The misery that flowed over her now in icy waves was her own fault. She should never have allowed Michael to persuade her to go today, should never let him say he loved her. But a tiny voice deep within her would not be stilled; she wanted desperately to hear him say it, for she loved him. Tears, the only thing in the cold little room that were warm, slid down her cheeks.

"Why, Lord, why is it this way? Why do I feel so deeply if he is the wrong man for me? I want to follow You, to know Your plan for me. But I love Michael, even though I knew quite plainly today that he is not the right man for me. Why did I fall in love with the wrong man? I don't understand, I just don't understand!"

Finally, slowly, even her tears grew cold as she huddled beneath the bedclothes; the day died just as slowly outside. As the night began—the long, cold night she was to remember only disjointedly later—Brenna was haunted by snatches of happy memories: Michael slipping the Claddaugh ring onto her finger, the peaceful lunch at Ardilaun House, the lovely ferry ride, the walk on the haunted, mysterious Inishmaan; the touch of the wedding lace on her hair...and Michael's arm around her, his lips on her own.

And then the sound of her own rejection of him came echoing back. "No, Michael, I can't...I can't marry you." The scenes whirled into a confusing jumble in her mind as troubled sleep edged her consciousness away. But sleep brought only a nightmare of cold confusion with the ever present knowledge that although she had never in her life loved anyone as she did Michael, she could never be his wife. The night seemed endless, and when morning came, dull and gray with no promise of sunshine, Brenna had unknowingly thrown back the down comforter and flannel sheets in her fitful sleep.

When at the prompting of a worried Seamus, Molly

opened Brenna's door quietly and saw the sleeping girl, she was alarmed at her flushed face and shallow breathing, which could be clearly heard across the room. Quickly she crossed the room and placed her hand on Brenna's cheek.

"Good heavens," she murmured, "her temperature must be at least a hundred and three."

Seamus was waiting discreetly but impatiently at the door. "What is it, Moll? What's wrong? By the Lord Harry, it's going on nine o'clock. She never made a sound, and I had to fix my own tea—" At the flash of warning on Molly's face he became contrite. "She certainly must be ill. Is it the influenza, would you guess?"

Molly nodded. "Yes, I would say so. But we'd best call Duffy right away to make certain." A sudden little moan from the bed made her retrace her steps. Brenna was shivering, her arms hugging her body as she drew herself into a tight little ball. "She's having chills now. Where are the extra comforters, Seamus? Would you get them for me, and call the doctor, and set the kettle on to boil? I'm going to have my hands full here."

The woeful expression on Seamus's face spoke volumes; Molly could read the thoughts there quite clearly. Not only would he have to fix his own breakfast, he was to be at Molly's beck and call as well. He started down the hall, then came back to stand in the door, his eyes on Brenna, who was making a small whimpering noise. "She's a sweet lassie, isn't she, Molly?"

"Yes, it's a grand girl she is." She smoothed Brenna's dark hair back with a gentle hand.

At her touch Brenna opened her eyes and murmured, "Michael?"

"No, dear, it's Molly." She sat on the edge of the bed. "Lie still, my dear. I think perhaps you've caught the influenza from Seamus."

163

Brenna's eyes seemed very large and dark in the paleness of her face. "Oh, Molly, he said he loves me." Molly nodded, he lower lip caught in her teeth. "He asked me to marry him and...and I can't!" She moaned and shivered, and Molly drew the covers up over her shoulders.

"Hush, child. There'll be time later to worry about all that. I'm very much afraid you've quite a bout ahead of you." A muffled sort of growl from the doorway made her look up. "Oh, Seamus. I thought you'd gone. The blankets—"

His brows knit together in the old familiar scowl. "Sure and I'll get them, and I'll make the tea, and the call. Blinking servant, that's what I am."

Molly correctly divined his gruffness as stemming from worry, not real ill temper. So she scolded quietly, "Now, Seamus, you old goat, get along with you. She'll be fine, I'm sure of it. She's a strong, healthy girl." He finally nodded and shuffled away, his lame leg stiff from his confinement. And Molly added to herself what she had not said to Seamus, *It's not the influenza that will get her down, it's her broken heart...*She watched helplessly as the tears seeped one by one, slowly and inexorably from Brenna's tightly shut eyes.

Later, when Dr. Duffy came in response to Seamus's worried call, his diagnosis concurred with Molly's. He took her aside after his examination of Brenna. "She's going to be a sick young woman for a few days. I talked to Michael, saw him in the village on my way, and he told me they were caught in the rain. She was soaked to the skin and must have been quite chilled." He looked at Molly keenly. "There's something more than a chill in this, sure as the world."

For a moment she weighed the problem of breaking confidence, then decided Dr. Duffy should know.

Molly nodded, her hands jammed in her apron pocket. "I gather Michael proposed, when they were over on the island, and she refused."

"Oh, well, he's not every woman's cuppa, for all his good looks." Dr. Duffy tugged his waistcoat over his ample middle. "He's a lot like Seamus, and as I recall, you—"

Molly cut him off. "I'm afraid she cares deeply for Michael, but in spite of that she felt she mustn't marry him. There were other considerations."

"Bother. So my patient is lovesick as well as very sick indeed with influenza. That might makes things even worse."

Molly drew a deep breath. "That's why I thought I should tell you, even though t'is a very private matter."

The doctor scowled, and though his face was smooth shaven and his brows rather finely drawn, his expression was remarkably like that of his old friend Seamus. "We must take great care to insure that she does not contract pnemonia."

"Yes. I'll do all I can," said Molly, with a worried glance at Brenna, who had again tossed the covers from her fevered body. "Excuse me, Duff, I must see to her."

"Hmmmm. She's fortunate to have you here, Molly. I've heard from many a recovered patient that you're a dab hand at nursing."

"I'll surely do my best here, Duff. The girl has m' heart." Molly's voice was quiet as she went to cover Brenna, leaving Dr. Duffy standing in the doorway.

"I'd say you're not the only one. Seamus was scared silly for her when he called me. Even the people in the village all speak well of her. My wife says she's 'a darlin' girl'—her own words, mind you—and Jimmy Flood is still singing her praises every time I pop in there. And then there's Michael."

"Yes, there's Michael," said Molly with a shake of her head. "Sure, and it's sorry I am that they are both so unhappy. I tried to warn her...I just cannot say how it will all turn out. Duff, will you make certain Seamus has plenty of aspirin?"

"We do."

She turned quickly at the quiet words; it was Michael. Duffy turned and placed a hand on the younger man's shoulder, gave a sympathetic squeeze, and left. Hesitantly Michael walked over to where Brenna lay, her eyes closed in a restless sleep. He stared down at the loose, dark hair and the pale face unhappy even in sleep, and Molly's eyes saw the misery in his own face. "She'll be all right, Michael. She's young and strong, and she'll recover very soon."

"And will she recover from what I did to her, what I said on the island? Molly, I'd promised her!"

"Promised her what?" Molly kept her voice low; Brenna stirred in her sleep and moved restlessly at the sound of Michael's passionate words. "Perhaps we'd best move over there, so as not to waken her." She inclined her head to the window seat.

Michael nodded, but he stood looking down at Brenna for a long while before he allowed Molly to take his arm and lead him to the other side of the room. His voice was low and without expression when he finally spoke, slumped against the faded blue cushions. "I'd promised not to talk about it, not to...not to touch her, take her in my arms..." His voice broke, and he put a hand wearily over his eyes.

"Michael, you don't have to be explaining this to me." Molly placed a gentle hand on Michael's bowed head.

"But, don't you see, Molly, I can't explain it! She seemed so—it seemed as though she—" For all his

166

brashness, Michael halted, unable to go on.

Molly finished his statement. "She seemed to feel the same as you did."

"Yes. Perhaps I wanted for her to so badly." He looked at Molly squarely now. "But no, Molly, she even told me she loved me, *she said she loved me.*" He clenched his fists on his knees in fury.

"And I believe she meant it with all her heart, Michael dear."

"But that makes no sense at all. I was not wanting to compromise her, Molly, I asked her to be my wife!"

"Did she give you no reason for her refusal?"

"Yes, she started talking about her God," he said almost viciously. "I don't understand."

Molly's look was keen and direct. "You say you love her."

"I do, I swear it!"

"Do you love her enough to try to understand why she refused?"

"I..." For a moment the old angry rebellion was plain in his dark eyes, but a muffled moan brought them both their feet. "Yes, Molly, I must. I cannot let her go. I cannot."

"Then we'll speak of it later. But for now we must do whatever is necessary to insure she gets better as quickly as possible. Agreed?" She smiled and laid a hand on his weary face. "You've not shaved, lad. Did you sleep a'tall last night?"

A smile twitched the corner of his mouth. "I hear the Mum in your tone, Moll."

"Go along with you. Bring the girl and me some tea, and some juice if you've any about the place. And if you don't, go and get some. The fever is likely to go high."

Obediently he went to the door, but his hand clutched the door frame as though he were loathe to

167

leave. "It's my fault she's fallen ill."

"Hush, none of that. Go on with you now."

For Brenna the next few days and nights were filled with a steady procession of demands that she drink this, and take that, and rest quietly, all of which she did obediently and in almost total silence. She seemed to almost welcome the awful ache in her bones, the raging fever, the pain in her chest, for then she could not think about that day on the island. She did ask Molly to call her father. Later she asked about her plane reservations to return to the States and was told by Molly they'd been cancelled until further notice.

Until further notice. She floated on a sea of pain and disjointed dreams. When she was asleep Michael's dark eyes and mocking smile haunted her, when she was awake he was often there by her bed, a damp cloth at the ready to wipe her brow, her wrists. His touch was always gentle, but there were times when the look in his eyes was more than she could bear. She had no strength to face him, and more often than not she would pull away and turn from him, unable to bear the storm in her heart. He would sit quietly for what seemed an eternity; then she'd hear him rise and leave the room. And no matter how desperately she wanted to call him back, she bit her lips savagely and waited until she heard him to down the stairs before giving way to the helpless, noiseless sobbing that was all the more painful for its silence.

It was raining. Brenna heard the drops against the window, knew there was a wind as well because of the force of their striking, and the sound made her feel as cold and lonely as her thoughts. *I have stayed too long in this place. I came to Ireland to search for peace and found war. I came to Ireland to search for my family and instead I find myself reaching out to strangers. I came to Ireland to look for my own peculiar will-o-the-wisp, that of a simple, long-ago kind of life which vanished from my world so many years ago that it exists only in the minds of the old ones, and in the minds of those like me. Those who are dissatisfied with the frantic quality of their lives, who yearn for quiet, less hurried days...such as I have experienced since I came to Crosswinds. And I can't stay, I can't.*

The sure knowledge only brought more bitter tears.

Finally, she began to mend. Dr. Duffy, on his usual daily visit, pronounced it so himself. He took the thermometer from her mouth, scrutinized it closely, and said, "Good, good. Normal for the second day in a row now."

"But why do I feel so weak, Dr. Duffy?" Brenna asked, quite self-conscious at the sight of Seamus, Molly, and Michael lined up to hear Duffy's verdict.

Duffy gave a snort that sounded very much like his friend Seamus at his best. "Sure, and you've been very ill, lass. Whatever did you expect?"

Meekly she answered, "Yes, I suppose you're right. But there must be something I can do to get stronger faster. You've all been wonderful, but you can't take care of me forever. And I have to think about going—"

Michael broke in then. "She's right, Duff. There must be something we can do to help her get better."

"Of course there is. Good, nourishing food—"

"I'll be happy to continue bringing in food for as long as is needed," put in Molly.

"—plenty of rest, and it wouldn't hurt for her to soak up some of that warm summer sun before it goes away, as indeed it is sure to do," finished Duffy, quite as

169

though Molly had never said a word.

"I'll see to that," said Michael.

Dr. Duffy and Molly walked out together, heads close in conversation about the invalid's diet. Seamus followed, saying woefully, "And I suppose it's up to me to keep on makin' the tea." He gave a huge, overdone sigh and threw back at Brenna, "But you're worth it, lass, sure and you're worth it!"

Michael came over to the bed, and before Brenna divined his intent, he wrapped her snugly in the finely knitted afghan and scooped her up into his arms.

"Michael, what are you doing?"

"Taking you for a bit of sun, as Duffy said."

"But I can walk," she said faintly, partly because she was still quite weak and partly because she thought she could not bear the closeness of him.

"Don't argue. I've some time on my hands, and if you—" He took a deep breath and continued, "—if you like, I'd be happy to read to you."

"I'd like that very much," she said honestly. Her hands had quite naturally curled around his neck; the thick dark hair there was crisp and clean feeling.

"What would you like to hear?" He glanced at the small table beside the bed. "Those are yours, I take it?" When she nodded he bent and picked the two top volumes from the pile and dropped them into her lap, then moved easily out of the room as though she were weightless. As he descended the stairs under the knowing glances of Seamus and Duffy in the hallway he said, "You've lost weight, lass. You're no heavier than thistledown."

"I suppose that's good if you insist on carrying me," she murmured against his shoulder.

He maneuvered out the back door, through the carefully tended herb garden and on to the outer garden.

170

There he settled her on a slatted oak bench just the other side of the gazebo, tucking the afghan snugly around her again. Then he sat beside her and leaned his head back. "This was a capital idea. The sun is absolutely marvelous, isn't it."

"Oh, yes." Brenna breathed deeply; the warm, flower-scented air was heavenly after being shut up indoors so long. "Thank you for bringing me out."

"My pleasure," he said gruffly.

Something in his tone sent a shaft of panic into her. "Michael, I don't—"

He held up both hands to stop her. "Not to worry. I'm not going to say or do anything that would disturb you, doctor's orders." He picked up the books from where he'd laid them on the bench. "Not a wide choice. Irish history or the Bible. What's your pleasure, Miss?"

"You decide. Or you don't have to read at all," she said quietly. "You haven't mentioned the puppy lately. Have you named her?"

"No." He stared at the two books in his hands. "I thought perhaps you'd help me think of a name."

Brenna couldn't keep from smiling as a thought struck her. "How about Guinevere?"

He glanced at her, then after a long pause said, "We'll call her Gwen for now. She's really rather small for the whole thing. Guinevere. I like it."

"Well, I was thinking of Lancelot...." She trailed off, struck silent by the easy intimacy between them so quickly recovered.

"I'll bring her up to see you later. She's taken up residence on Seamus's footstool." He put one of the books down. "Irish history is more than I can take on a day like today."

Brenna nodded; the afternoon was indeed beautiful. The phlox were in full bloom, and their scent mingled

171

and wove a wonderful tapestry of odors with the roses and heather. Vaguely she thought of the honeysuckle at home in Texas. The fragrance was delightful and heady stuff, of which Brenna drank deeply, quite the same as she would clear water from a mountain stream. She closed her eyes and listened idly to the faint rustle of the thin India paper of her Bible.

"Why, you've written in your Bible!" Michael's voice was shocked. "Why ever did you do that?"

"You were probably taught never to write in a book," Brenna said with a laugh.

"I most certainly was. And a Bible...that's even worse, it seems."

"A lot of people feel that way, I suppose. But an old preacher taught me to do it and said he always had. So I underline and make little notes, and it helps me remember things."

He'd stopped turning pages. "You read it every day, then?"

There was no mistaking the quiet interest in his tone. "Yes, except since I've been sick my eyes don't always cooperate. At times they almost seemed to cross, and I just gave up trying."

Michael laughed softly. "I'll read then, here where you've underlined." He drew a deep breath, audible clearly in the soft summer air, and began. " 'God is love. Whoever lives in love lives in God, and God in him. Love is made complete among us so that we will have confidence on the day of judgment, because in this world we are like him. There is no fear in love. But perfect love drives out fear, because fear has to do with punishment. The man who fears is not made perfect in love.' "

For a long, long moment he was silent, then he said, so low that Brenna could hardly make out the words,

"I'm afraid...there are times I'm afraid and I don't even know of what...."

She held her breath. Something told her this was not the right time to speak to Michael, to tell him how much God loved him and wanted him to live without fear. So she only said, "That was lovely. You have a good voice for reading aloud. Would you...do you mind reading some more? I never get tired of hearing it, no matter how many times I've read it, or had it read to me."

He finished reading the fourth chapter, and the next, then sat quietly for a long while. Brenna followed his example. She asked God to speak to Michael's heart, to bring him closer to Himself...and to her surprise realized she was praying quite unselfishly. When the sun suddenly hid itself behind a capricious cloud, Michael roused and said, "Perhaps I'd best carry you in before a soft Irish rain comes to undo all the good of the sun. May I carry you in, lass?"

The look in his eyes was different than she had ever seen; humble, it was, and entreating. "I...thank you, Michael, you're very considerate."

"Perhaps. And perhaps I only enjoy holding you in my arms." His touch held nothing but solicitude—no passion or desire to make Brenna anxious. When he put her on her bed, which had by a small Molly miracle been straightened and looked fresh and inviting once more, he said quietly, "I'll see you later, and I'll bring Gwen. There's something I must speak to Molly about." He stood silently, looking down at her, for a long while, then without another word turned and left.

She lay still, her mind and spirit feeling a most extraordinary peace. Nothing was different; Michael was still far from being the right man for her as ever, regardless of his gentleness today. But somehow the familiar words from 1 John had done their work. She had no fear of the future, even though that future did not include Michael Larkin. Perhaps the healing sun had soothed the pain, perhaps God in his own mysterious way was healing her heart as well as her body. Whatever the reason, she slept the afternoon away, to awaken that evening ravenously hungry and ready for Molly's excellent supper. She was indeed on the mend.

Chapter Fourteen

July was much as June had been; the days flowed easily
with fine bright sunshine, but never so much and so
harsh that the forty shades of lovely green faded. The
soft Irish rain came and went, and with its benevolent
frequency the hay in the fields round about grew to impressive heights, and the flowers in the wonderfully
wild garden flourished each in their time. The weeks
were a period of deceptively simple pleasure for
Brenna, a time when she assumed only part of the du-
ties she'd had before her illness. Because Nola had in-
formed her mother that Brenna was filling in for her,
Mrs. O'Malley sent word of her intention to "bide a bit
longer" at her sister's. No one thought to tell her the
new help was ill.

Seamus grumbled, but plainly he did not begrudge
Brenna the time he spent doing "women's work." But
the day came when Brenna knew she could no longer
put off her plans to leave. She and Michael were very
polite to each other, and he had not, since the day he'd
carried her into the garden and read to her, made even
so much as a casual reference to their earlier impas-
sioned, painful encounters. Their love was over, her
mind told her, and her mind also told her that was for
the best. Yet every time he came banging in the back
door, or when he came quietly into a room without her

seeing, her heart felt his presence...knew he was there.

He was out on a call now, and she decided to make certain the account books were completely in order. But first she forced herself to contact the travel agent in Galway and arrange for her flight home. When her call was done, her flight was booked for Tuesday, just four days away, out of Shannon International Airport. She sat numbly for a time, telling herself there was nothing else she could do. She was uncertain about her job in Houston, even though her father, in several long, outrageously expensive phone calls, had assured her he'd spoken to her boss and explained the situation fully. He and Celia had even talked of flying over to bring her home, but she'd convinced him that she was fine and they should wait until they could make the long, leisurely visit he'd always wanted, instead of a hurry-up emergency one.

Her job...her quiet, elegant apartment...her very life seemed to stretch lonely and empty without Seamus and Michael, and the pleasant chaos of Crosswinds. Only the thought that somehow with God's help she would find something better enabled her to face the prospect of leaving.

Resolutely she spent the better part of the next hour checking each column of figures. When the kitchen door banged noisily she was still sitting at the graceful little desk in the parlor. She called without thinking, chagrined at her eagerness. "Michael, is that you?"

A short laugh told her it was Nola before the red-haired girl breezed into the room, saying, "No, luv, it's not Michael. Sorry to disappoint you!" Same as always, Brenna thought; her bright red hair was flying, her fists akimbo as she surveyed Brenna and the books spread all around. "Still slaving away for those two clever rascals?" She shook her head knowingly. "They've got you hoodwinked entirely and completely."

"I do it because I want to," Brenna answered a little stiffly. Then she saw something in Nola's eyes that made her suspect the girl was far from the same after all. "Has something happened, Nola? Are you all right?"

"Of course I'm all right!" she snapped, eyes blazing. "What makes you think you can read my mind?" Suddenly her face crumpled. Her eyes closed tightly, but she couldn't hold back the sudden tears. She reached blindly behind her and sank into the nearest chair.

Brenna came over to her and without thinking dropped to her knees beside the chair, a sympathetic hand on Nola's arm. "What is it?" She watched helplessly as Nola, who prided herself on her strength, her toughness, gave way to a flood of tears. When they subsided somewhat Brenna asked softly, "It's Sean, isn't it?"

Wearily Nola nodded. "They've got him, they put him in jail, and tomorrow he's to be taken to London, and they won't let me see him, and I'll *die* if I don't!"

Because she knew better than to deny that passionate statement Brenna merely soothed, "Surely they'll let you see him in time, Nola."

"In time? *Time?* You act as if my Sean and me have plenty! Our time is *gone....*" Her tearstained face held such pain that the emotion-charged words rang true, despite their drama.

"I'm sure that's not so, Nola."

"Well, I'm not sure at all." Nola grew quiet then, with a faraway look in her eyes. "There's talk among the prisoners of a hunger strike. If...if they begin, Sean will see it to the end, I know it. He's not a man to go halfway."

Brenna did not doubt it. She couldn't imagine Nola being attracted to a weak-minded man. "It's a difficult situation, and I'm sorry that you have to face it."

Nola's eyes finally focused on Brenna. "You mean that, don't you?"

"Yes, I do."

A look of uncertainty, rare for Nola, crossed her face. "You're a puzzlement to me. Somehow you're…you're different, and I'm not a'tall certain what makes the difference."

Quietly Brenna said, "I can tell you, Nola. It's really very simple. The difference you see is not anything I can take credit for. It's God in me." For a moment she held her breath; the look of longing on Nola's face to know more spoke volumes of her inner struggle.

But Nola almost visibly shoved her longing aside. "Ah, I've no time for religious folderol. There was enough of that when I was under me Mum's thumb." Still, something in her eyes made Brenna know that when the time was right and Nola's need was strong enough, she would ask again.

"Well, if you ever want to talk about it, I'd be more than willing to listen, and tell you my own experiences. As for Sean, I know how it is when you love someone and…"

"Michael." The one quiet word dropped like a stone in calm water. For a time Brenna could not reply. The ripples of emotion that went through her prevented speech. "Has he told you he loves you?" asked Nola, kindly for her. Brenna nodded. "But he has not proposed, I take it." As quickly her voice was shrewd and knowing.

"As a matter of fact, he did," murmured Brenna. "But I had to tell him no."

"What?" Nola's expression was incredulous. "You can't mean that you refused him? *Why*?"

"Because…" Brenna could not think how to explain her heart to this girl. She could not understand, as Michael himself had not understood. So she said simply, "He was not the right man for me, Nola."

"You're daft," Nola said bluntly. "And so why are you still here?"

"I've been ill."

Nola saw now what she hadn't before, Brenna's pale face and thin body. "Seamus's influenza, I'll wager. That's been a good excuse to hang about, luv, for I'm certain you've reconsidered and are just waiting for Michael to ask you again."

"Nola, I'm not doing any such thing!"

"Rubbish. You aren't as stupid as you seem. If he asks you again, I'll bet a pretty you'd say yes. Am I right?"

Both Brenna, who hadn't the least notion as to what to say, and Nola were startled at Michael's voice from the doorway. "I'd like to hear the answer to that question myself."

"Oh, Michael, they've taken Sean! He's been arrested, and I'm that worried!" exclaimed Nola, characteristically forgetting Brenna's problems entirely.

"Not good," said Michael with a frown. "Have you seen him?"

"No, and they say they'll not allow it." For a moment her shoulders slumped, then the natural toughness inherent in her makeup took over. "But I will never give up trying to see him and set him free. And where is the old man? I want to see him, that's why I came."

Brenna hesitated, then decided she had nothing to lose. "Nola, remember, if you need someone to talk to, I'll be—"

"You'll be in America, remember?" Nola said with a malicious grin. "What's to keep you here if Michael can't? Poor Michael, lost your touch, have you?"

"Nola, how can you?" Brenna burst out.

"How can *I*? It would seem, luv, that *you* won our little wager."

"What wager is that?" asked Michael.

Brenna bit her lip. "Nola, please don't—"

"Don't what? Tell Michael that the first time I laid eyes on you—in me own bed, as I recall, you took over right off like you owned the place—we had a chatty little visit and I bet you couldn't make our laddie Michael take a tumble for you. Sure now, and you remember that?"

Brenna felt her face grow warm as Michael stared at her in disbelief. "Michael, it wasn't like that at all."

"Then exactly how was it?"

"Exactly as I said," Nola answered. "As for me payin' up, I'm a bit short at the moment. But the satisfaction of knowing you brought our Michael to his knees and then refused him should be enough pay. My hat's off to you, lass. You're probably smart to turn him down. He's a bad risk for a husband, he is." She drew a deep breath and her face showed the sudden pain she felt. "Although I must admit I'm not a better chooser meself. Ah, Sean…"

Michael put an arm around her shoulders as he walked her to the door. "Seamus is in the back, tending a patient. He'll be glad to see you. And…and if I can help, I'm here."

Nola swallowed visibly at the kindness in his tone. "Thank you, Michael. I may need you."

"To hear you admit it may be a milestone," remarked Michael without rancor as he watched her swing down the hall. Then he turned slowly and came back to where Brenna stood at the front window. "Come for a walk with me?"

The quiet request made her next words even harder

to say. "Michael, I've made reservations to fly home for next Tuesday."

"I thought we'd go up Sky Road—as far as you're able."

"Michael, did you hear what I said?"

"I heard. Come with me?" His dark eyes held hers, and she found she could not break away from their compelling gaze. "We'll go slowly. I know you still aren't ready for a run."

She smiled. "I wasn't ready for that before I got sick."

Michael took her arm. "It's warm enough. You won't need a heavier sweater…if it does get cooler, I'll give you my jacket."

She nodded, not trusting herself to speak as she remembered that other day; it seemed so long ago, when he had put his jacket around her shoulders and kissed her for the first time. As though in a dream she moved slowly with him from the room.

In the hall they were intercepted by a thunderfaced Seamus and a defiant Nola. Seamus was growling, "And just what do you think you're about, young lady, making plans to leave without telling me? If it wasn't for Nola here, I would be in the dark entirely."

Brenna decided to tease him out of his mood if she could. "Why, Seamus, have I been here so long I need permission?"

"Permission? Bah! If you'd asked, I'd have said no. You're not strong enough. You should bide awhile longer....." He trailed off, not bothering to hide the woeful expression that replaced the thunder. "I've gotten used to having you about, girl. If you go, I'll be lonely for you."

Nola interrupted, pouting prettily, "Now, Seamus, am I not enough daughter for you?"

"Well, if the truth be told, you're a fine lassie and you

brighten up things considerable, but you're too often flittin' around. Now our Brenna here is a stay-at-home." He gave Brenna a beguiling smile. "You see how it is, don't you? Don't go making any hasty decisions about leaving us. For that matter, I don't see why you don't just...stay."

Brenna went to him and hugged him close. She doubted anyone did that often. For while Nola loved the old man dearly, she had almost as much difficulty as he did showing it. "Oh, Seamus, the time I've spent with you—flu and all—has been the most wonderful in my life. But...I can't stay." The last words were no more than a whisper, but Brenna knew from Michael's expression that he had heard. Seamus was silent. She held him close for a moment longer, then stepped back. "Michael and I are going for a walk. We may be gone for a while."

"Watch out for him, luv," said Nola. "You know, or maybe you don't, but you should, how these wild black Irishmen get when they're spurned."

Brenna glanced at Michael, half-expecting him to explode at Nola's taunting words. But he merely said, "Come, Brenna, let's not waste the sunshine. Nola, if you're gone when we get back, keep us abreast of the developments with Sean."

"Aye, that I will, Michael," she said, looking at him in surprise. He'd always risen to the bait before. She watched, a slightly puzzled look on her face as Michael gently steered Brenna out the front door.

He breathed deeply of the fresh summer air, then carefully guided Brenna down the main road. "I'm glad you're better."

"So am I. It feels marvelous to be outside again, moving under my own steam." Only a short distance down the road they saw Joey, cycling toward them without his donkey and cart this time, but with a dog trotting by his

182

side. He swung off his bicycle, obviously pleased to see them.

"And a good day to you both," he said cheerily. "I've not seen you about these many days."

"She's been ill, caught the influenza after she nursed Seamus through a bout," said Michael, his fingers unconsciously scratching the black and white dog who'd come to his side.

"Oh, and that's too bad, it is," said the man in total sympathy. "But you're better now, I take it?"

"I certainly am, and grateful, too," answered Brenna.

He and Michael chatted for a few moments longer. After he pedaled on, Michael said, his voice thoughtful, "It's really fine how everyone you meet seems to accept you, and like you enormously. You are an exceptional American tourist."

"I could have told you that," teased Brenna. They had walked only a short distance farther when she said regretfully, "I'm afraid I'm getting tired."

Immediately he murmured, a trifle wickedly, "I would be more than happy to carry you."

"But—" She broke off, realizing too late that he was teasing her. "You've done quite enough of that, I'd say."

"Or not near enough." They'd reached the low stone wall where Brenna had sat so long ago to survey Clifden for the first time. Michael removed his corduroy jacket, folded it carefully, and placed it on the stone. "Here, we'll sit for a spell."

They sat comfortably side by side, neither of them speaking, drinking in the hazy blue shapes of the Twelve Bens. Then Michael said, "I suppose the peat smoke makes them blue."

"Or the pure air...whatever it is, they're the loveliest sight I can imagine. They must have been a wonderful, comforting part of your childhood."

"They were my mountains," he said gravely. "As a boy I claimed them for my own."

"I've never had that pleasure. We have a hazy atmosphere over Houston most of the time, but some people say that it's the hazy smell of money."

"We're doing it again."

"Doing what?"

"Speaking of everything but what we're actually thinking of." He turned to face her. "Brenna, there are some things I must say to you."

"Please don't. We've said it all, and I don't think I can stand it again," she pleaded.

"You must listen—"

Suddenly she felt a welcome spurt of anger. "And what if I don't want to listen this time?"

"But I must tell you something very important."

She did not protest again, but the painful unfairness of the situation made her stiff and unyielding beside him. "Michael, you're making things worse. I've tried, honestly tried, to be fair and do the best I could in an impossible situation."

"That you have."

"Then why do you insist on dragging things out? It hurts me so...." Her words ended in a little wail and she clenched her jaws, willing herself not to cry; but he saw the shine of tears.

"Oh, Brenna darling, don't cry! I've hurt you enough already, and I love you so."

"Then just let me go, Michael, please?"

"I can't do that. I want you to stay and marry me."

She shook her head, one fist pressed tight against her lips. "I can't believe you want to hurt me like this!"

"That's the last thing I want. I'm sorry, I'm being unbelievably clumsy. Forgive me." He looked so woebegone Brenna almost weakened...almost.

184

With a slight edge of desperation in her voice she said, "Michael, nothing's different, things are still just the same. We shouldn't keep going over and over them."

"But you're wrong, Brenna," he said softly.

"Wrong? What do you mean?"

"Things are not the same. *I'm* not."

"I don't understand. Michael, if I explained my feelings badly, I'm sorry. The plain truth is, you are not the right man for me." There, she had said it again, finally and irrevocably. He couldn't argue any further.

"But Brenna, the man who tried to bully you, who thought he could by sheer force of will change your mind, is gone. I was so wrong, that day on the island ...it was wrong of me to force myself on you. But I wanted you, and I thought I could have what I wanted...." Slowly, he said, "I am no longer that willful man."

At his confusing words she jumped from the wall, and a lightheadedness made her sway. He was beside her instantly, his arms tight around her to prevent her from falling. "Please, let me go...."

"Don't you see that I'm a new man?"

She twisted upward to look into his face for the first time since they'd left the house. There was, indeed, something different about him. She tried to slow her shallow breathing and the rapid-fire beating of her heart. Yes, there was a calm and gentleness of spirit in his eyes that had not been there before. "Michael, tell me what has happened...something did happen, didn't it?"

He nodded. "The most significant thing in my life." She laid her head on his chest, and the deep resonance of his words rang softly in her head as he spoke. "For days, weeks, I suppose—I'm as confused about time

185

now as you probably are—I've been talking with Molly."

Brenna's throat tightened; she knew now what he was talking about. "Oh, Michael."

"She explained so many things that I'd heard before, but they'd meant nothing to me. And suddenly the verses of Scripture that I had ridiculed made perfect sense, perfect. I'm a new man now, a new man in Christ." His tone was hushed and full of awe.

Joyous laughter burst from Brenna as she threw her arms around his neck and hugged him tightly.

He laughed with her, and the sound was warm and close in her ear. "And now you know why I cannot let you go, why I can dare to ask again if you'll marry me." His voice was husky, and his lips brushed her hair, her cheek. "Say yes, Brenna, say yes, to this new man who loves you more than the old man could ever dream of!"

She raised her head and looked straight into his eyes, so full of love and peace now. "Yes, Michael, yes!" And now it was Brenna who pulled his head down to hers, Brenna who found his eager lips with her own and seemed unable to get enough of his kisses.

When at last the bright weather dimmed and a whisper of soft rain touched Michael's hair, then and only then did she pull away slightly. "We should be starting back, shouldn't we?"

He nodded and kissed her once more. "You certainly shouldn't get wet again. Are you cold?"

"Not much."

Immediately, solicitiously, he picked up his jacket, shook it out, and placed it around her shoulders. Something slipped to the ground, and Brenna saw that it was the tissue he'd wrapped the wedding veil in. "Oh, Michael, not again!"

He laughed a little as he stooped to pick it up. "Don't

worry, Brenna, Irish lace isn't as fragile as it looks. It's strong, and enduring, like…" He stopped, his expression uncertain. "I've always thought of myself as a plain speaking man, not…fanciful."

Brenna took the lace, touched it to her face. *He must have been carrying it with him since that day on the island*, she thought; there was the scent of his aftershave lingering faintly on it. "Tell me what you were going to say, Michael."

"Only that it's like my love for you."

"Strong and enduring," she said very softly.

"Yes. Let's go home, Brenna."

"Home." When *home* meant Crosswinds, Brenna thought it must be the most wonderful word possible.

"I want to tell Seamus that you'll not be leaving after all."

"And I want to tell Molly!"

"Ah, and I think Molly knows already," he said with a lift of one fine brow.

"She does? Were you that confident?"

Ruefully he said, "If the truth be told, no. But she has made me aware of so many things, among them a verse which says, 'With Christ all things are possible.' She did say, when I asked her what she thought my chances were with you, that she thought it highly unlikely you could resist me. I agreed with her."

Brenna laughed again. She could not seem to stop laughing. "It was hard enough before, you egotistical man, and impossible now."

He looked at her keenly. "As to that wager Nola mentioned. Did you really bet her you could make me fall in love with you?"

She blushed and looked back steadily. "It wasn't exactly like that. Nola was the one who said how attractive all the women find you."

"And you didn't find me attractive?"

"Oh, yes I did." The love in her eyes cleared away the last doubts; he reached for her again and she went gladly into his embrace. She smoothed the dark hair that curled at his neck. " 'All things are possible'...that means Seamus, too, and Nola..."

He held her at arm's length, shaking his head. "You and Molly are a fine pair—never leaving a man in peace." Then he said, with wonder in his voice, "No, that's not so at all. For the first time in my life I think I really know what peace is—and joy. You brought me joy, lass." When he drew her close again she felt it too, that joy he spoke of. And she knew it would last, because it was a shared joy, one that was theirs forever.

Dear Reader:

I am committed to bringing you the kind of romantic novels you want to read. Please fill out the brief questionnaire below so we will know what you like most in Cherish Romances_{TM}.

Mail to: Etta Wilson
Thomas Nelson Publishers
P.O. Box 141000
Nashville, Tenn. 37214

1. Why did you buy this Cherish Romance_{TM}?

☐ Author
☐ Back cover description
☐ Christian story
☐ Cover art
☐ Recommendation from others
☐ Title
☐ Other_____

2. What did you like best about this book?

☐ Heroine
☐ Hero
☐ Christian elements
☐ Setting
☐ Story Line
☐ Secondary characters

3. Where did you buy this book?

☐ Christian bookstore
☐ Supermarket
☐ Drugstore
☐ General bookstore
☐ Book Club
☐ Other (specify)_____

4. Are you interested in buying other Cherish Romances_{TM}?

   ☐ Very interested   ☐ Somewhat interested
                  ☐ Not interested

5. Please indicate your age group.
   ☐ Under 18   ☐ 25-34
   ☐ 18-24   ☐ 35-49   ☐ Over 50

6. Comments or suggestions?

7. Would you like to receive a free copy of the Cherish Romance_{TM} newsletter? If so, please fill in your name and address.

Name _____

Address _____

City _____ State _____ Zip _____

7350-1